# LOVE ACROSS THE WATER

The flooding of a Reithdale valley splits the farming community, and two families are drawn into a bitter feud. During a drought, when the old village and old memories are exposed, Jez Davies meets Martha Hetherington in the forgotten valley and falls in love. But Martha is unhappily married with a tiny baby and she and Jez find they are divided by more than the deep waters of the lake, as fate conspires to keep them apart.

*Books by Julia Clarke*
*in the Linford Romance Library:*

CRYSTA
FLOWER IN THE SNOW

JULIA CLARKE

# LOVE ACROSS THE WATER

*Complete and Unabridged*

**LINFORD**
*Leicester*

First Linford Edition
published 2000

British Library CIP Data

Clarke, Julia
  Love across the water.—Large print ed.—
  Linford romance library
  1. Love stories
  2. Large type books
  I. Title
  823.9'14 [F]

ISBN 0–7089–5700–5

Published by
F. A. Thorpe (Publishing)
Anstey, Leicestershire

Set by Words & Graphics Ltd.
Anstey, Leicestershire
Printed and bound in Great Britain by
T. J. International Ltd., Padstow, Cornwall

This book is printed on acid-free paper

# 1

Jez Davies threw back his shoulders and took a deep breath. Then, shielding his eyes with a large tanned hand, he surveyed the valley before him, noting the lowness of Throstlegill reservoir. The lake normally filled the valley with a sheet of blue water but now it was no more than a murky smudge of grey.

With a shake of his head Jez made his way quickly to a small copse of Scots pine which provided shade from the ferocity of the mid-day sun. It was hard to believe that this was an English summer, the great golden disk which burned down with such intensity from a flawless blue sky reminded him of a tropical sun.

When he was finally seated with his back against a tree he took his father's letter from his pocket and reread it. This letter had upset and shocked him more than his father's Will had done. Until his father's untimely death Jez had seen himself as unshakeable: at nearly thirty years old, a seasoned traveller, and well-known in his own field of work, he had seen himself as a mature man of the world. Now he realised that it had all been a veneer and that being able to cope with drought and famine in foreign countries, and take photographs which could make the world sit up and take notice, had not prepared him for the unexpected and terrible in his personal life. He felt confused and unhappy in a way which took him back to his early teenage years — the years after his mother had left.

The letter was short and to the point. '*Dear Jeremy*' (His father had never liked the shortened version of his name. Jez realized with a rueful smile that the last person in the world to call him Jeremy had gone — now he would always be Jez) '*By the time you read this letter you will know how*

*I have settled my financial affairs. I imagine you will be annoyed with me. You always liked everything to be fair and will think I haven't done right by your sisters. But they are all married well and amply provided for. I don't know if you will keep Beckwith Farm, it's yours now to do what you want with. I expect you are thinking that I have left it to you intact because I don't want it sold or split up. I have to admit that an old man's pride made me dream of my grandchildren playing in the garden and keeping ponies in the paddock but it's your life, Jeremy. If you do decide to sell then do so with a clear conscience. If however you decide to keep the farm I have a confession to make . . . '* At this point Jez stopped reading and looked up, his eyes searching the opposite hillside. The day was almost unnaturally still: the heat had driven the song birds into the thickets and the skylarks into the grass, so the only sign of life was a kestrel hovering in the distance.

'Oh Dad,' he said with a sigh. 'What have you landed me with?' He then proceeded with the letter. '*I have been proud of the work I have done at Beckwith Farm. But there is one thing I regret and that is the flooding of the valley to make the reservoir. It was false pride which stopped me ever admitting it — that and knowing it could never be undone. I made a lot of money from the project but others didn't. There has been bad feeling between valley folk who years ago were friends. I can't put it right, but maybe you can. Will you try for me, Jeremy? It is my dying wish that where there are now enemies there should be friends. It is the Hetheringtons who were hurt the most. I never see them, if I walk into the market and Hetherington is there he leaves immediately. Maybe you can heal the breech between us. I hope and pray so. God bless, son. Your loving father.*

Jez folded the letter, put it back in the envelope and rammed it almost savagely into his pocket. Then he made his way slowly back to Beckwith Farm, kicked at the dried summer grass, deep in thought. His sister Lydia was fussing in the kitchen, emptying the dishwasher and tidying cupboards: 'Why on earth have you been walking in this heat? You must be absolutely frazzled. Would you like some home-made lemonade?' she asked with all the familiar bossiness of an older sister.

'Yes please . . . ' he said peeking under a cloth on the table and taking a warm biscuit to eat. 'You are spoiling me, Lyd,' he said affectionately.

Lydia placed a glass and jug in front of him. 'Have you thought about what you are going to do? You don't have to stay here, you know. Allan has been running the farm on his own for months.'

'We'll have to get him some help. He's a first rate manager, but it's a waste to have him doing too many menial jobs when he could be putting his energy into building up the stock.'

'Yes, yes . . . ' Lydia said, a little impatiently. 'You're talking as if you've already decided what to do. Building up the stock hardly matters if you are going to sell.'

'I haven't decided what to do yet.' Jez said moodily. 'At first I was sure. I've never wanted to be a farmer and living here in Reithdale has never appealed to me. But now I don't know . . . the only thing I know for sure is not to make a decision in a hurry.'

'But what are you going to do for the time being? Surely you don't want to stay here on your own? Why don't you come home with me? Harry would love some company and the children are desperate to see you.' Lydia was frowning anxiously and Jez realized that she was missing her husband and family and, like a mother hen, wanted to take him home and have her brood safely tucked up together.

'I'll be fine here on my own, Dad managed. You get yourself home,

Lydia. I shan't starve or burn the house down. In fact I've only got a few weeks before I'm due to go to Nepal, it will be good thinking time.'

'I don't really know what there is to think about. You don't like farming and you have a wonderful career.' Lydia was suddenly irritable with him. He smiled and changed the subject:

'Do you ever see the Hetheringtons?' he asked.

'Good grief! No.' Lydia was shocked. 'Why on earth do you ask?'

'Just wondered,' Jez said with a shrug. 'They are our nearest neighbours.'

'Well, they were, until the valley was flooded. Now it's miles around to their side of the lake.'

'Were we ever friendly with them?' he asked.

'Oh no,' Lydia said dismissively. 'Dad and Hetherington used to borrow and lend, to help each other out, as farmers do: but they were never friends . . . The family were a real gaggle; hordes of scruffy children, all with their own sheep-dog puppies on bits of string.'

Jez burst out laughing. 'Honestly, Lyd, you are such a snob.' He leaned back in his chair and closed his eyes to shut out his sister's pouting face. Searching through his memory he had a distant recollection of a meeting with the Hetheringtons. 'We saw them once at Otley market,' he said suddenly. 'Mr Hetherington had ginger whiskers, there were lots of carrot-haired children and a baby.'

'There was a scene that afternoon,' Lydia said flatly. 'They were still very sore about the valley being flooded.'

'Why?' he asked. 'They would have got compensation same as Dad.'

'Oh, I don't know . . . Dad's share of the valley wasn't very good quality land. But the Hetherington's lost most of their pasture. People quarrel about such peculiar things . . .' Lydia said airily.

'If Dad had said no to the reservoir

would it have made a difference?' Jez asked musingly.

'I don't imagine so . . . ' Lydia said. 'I expect there would have been a compulsory purchase. I don't know why he let it bother him. The Hetheringtons are no loss . . . what does it matter if they don't talk to us? It's certainly never affected me.'

'How many of them are there?' Jez asked.

'Two boys, both abroad now I believe. A girl, Ruth, who is my age, she lives in Scotland. I see her in Harrogate sometimes when she's visiting. And then there's the baby — Martha — she's the arty one who lives in London.'

'And does old man Hetherington still run the farm?'

'Yes, he never looks any older. I see him at the Yorkshire Show. I don't think he knows who I am. His whiskers are grey now . . . '

'I'll call and see him sometime,' Jez said, rising to his feet, suddenly dynamic.

'Oh, I really shouldn't bother . . .' Lydia cried. 'There's nothing to be gained from it.' Jez wondered why he didn't show her the letter, but something stopped him. It was as if he and Dad had made a pact of honour about something which she would not understand. Lydia fussed a little more about what food was in the freezer and then left, shouting out an invitation for Sunday lunch as she did so. Fond though he was of his sister it was a relief when her Volvo disappeared down the drive in a little cloud of dust and he was alone at Beckwith Farm, alone with his memories and his father's instructions.

★ ★ ★

Martha found that driving through the night had one advantage — it was cool. London had been like a dust-bowl for weeks and, despite her misery, her spirits instinctively lifted as she sped away from the capital and felt the soft night wind on her tear-stained cheeks. Luke, snug in his carrier, slept sweetly, lulled by the continuous motion of the vehicle. She stopped at a motorway services just after midnight and gave him a drink, then she drove on through the darkness. Like a wounded animal she wanted to get to a place of safety to hide herself from the light of day and the inquisitive eyes of the world.

Her father was cooking his breakfast when Martha arrived at the farm. He looked up, his grey eyebrows raising quizzically at the sight of her, but he did not rush into a torrent of questions — it wasn't his way: 'Come and sit down, our lass,' he said kindly, holding out large gentle hands for the baby. 'Mam's still asleep. You must have left home early — you're up with the lark.'

'I haven't been to bed. I drove through the night,' she said quietly. Her father sucked in his cheeks, which she knew meant he was thinking hard. Then he said slowly, 'Well, you'll be tired and in need of breakfast, sit thyself down while I fry up some bacon.' She knew he was upset because his Dalesman's accent became more pronounced when he was emotional but he didn't ask any questions, apart from guidance about the baby's bottle. She and the child were like two of his orphan lambs, in need of tender loving care and food, and that was enough for now. He fed the baby expertly, with the child resting easily in the crook of his large arm, while she wolfed down bacon and eggs and then a round of doorstep toast. Finishing the meal with a sigh of contentment she realised she hadn't eaten for twenty four hours but had existed all that time on tension and black coffee.

'Have you much in the car? Shall I bring in your bag and the baby's sleeping-cot?' her father asked and it was then her control gave way.

'The car is packed to the roof with anything I could get in. I've left Toby, Dad. And I'm not going back.' Her voice was low with a sob rising in her throat and she couldn't bring herself to say any more.

Her father avoided her eyes as he said levelly: 'Well then, I'd best get it all unpacked for you. Babe is nearly asleep. When you've got him settled why don't you have forty winks? I'm just about to take Mam a cup of tea. I'll tell her you're abed and to wake you later in the morning.'

Rising he moved to the door, but, as he drew level with her, he bent and kissed her face, an awkward peck on her forehead. 'What ever happens, our lass, you know you always have a home here with us. Your bed's made up and ready.'

After he had left the kitchen, Martha brushed tears from her eyes with the back of her hand. Her bed was made up and ready. It spoke volumes. Her room had never been changed, never allowed to be used by visiting grandchildren. It still contained her college books, her art folders and an enormous cork-board covered with pictures and sketches which dated from her school days.

There had never been a family row about her marrying Toby. No one had ever whispered the words, 'wild and unsuitable', but in her heart she had known that her parents were never entirely happy with her choice of mate. Toby was like an exotic foreign bird who had swooped down on a very ordinary dove-cote, seduced a small shy henbird, and whisked her away to far-off and dangerous places. When she was a little girl and had been prone to temper tantrums her father had often predicted the outcome of too much excitement: 'It'll end in tears . . . ' he would warn. Well, he had been right about her headlong flight into matrimony with Toby. She hadn't known it was possible to cry so much; she had cried her self sick and faint, she had cried herself angry and pathetic in turn, and finally she had cried herself home.

With a sigh she rose to her feet

and laid the sleeping baby over her shoulder. Her room was ready, her bed was made up. Maybe her parents had always known that one day she would need it again.

Sleep eluded her. She showered and lay on her bed staring at the ceiling. At eleven o'clock her mother brought her tea and toast and she pretended she had been dozing. All day she stayed in the indoors, unpacking and caring for the baby. There was a feeling of almost palpable expectation in the house: her mother was waiting for her to talk about what had happened and she was waiting for the phone to ring.

In the cool of the evening, when Luke was bathed and put to bed, she faced her parents as they sat around the supper table. 'I'm not going back to Toby. I am going to divorce him,' she said. 'I'll tell you about it when I feel I can — but not now . . . ' Looking at their sorrowful faces her own expression hardened. 'I'm sorry . . . ' she whispered. They sat in silence for a few moments, then she rose to her feet. 'I think I'll take those two puppies of yours for a walk, Dad. I could do with some fresh air.'

Without thinking she walked over the hill and down to the water. She knew now that Toby was not going to phone, not tonight, not ever. Craving comfort she wanted to look at the lake; she had always loved the sweep of blue water nestling between the hillsides and she felt sure that sitting beside the still waters would soothe her heavy heart.

As she came through the thicket of trees which shielded the lake from the house her eyes widening with astonishment and her footsteps quickened as she took in the full meaning of the sight before her eyes. The lake had all but disappeared and the whole familiar landscape of her childhood had changed. She unclipped the dogs' leads and they set off in mad circles scenting rabbits and water rats but she rushed on, walking quickly, almost running. She was moving over land which before had always been covered with water but which now was cracked and baked hard and she did not stop until she reached the water's edge. 'It's coming back,' she whispered. 'It's coming back to us.'

She burst into the kitchen, the puppies at her heels, her hair flying in a wild auburn curtain behind her. Her mother looked up from the her knitting, her face started: 'What ever is the matter, Martha?'

'Mam, did you know that the lake is nearly dry. We'll soon be able to see the old village and the farm!' she cried impetuously.

'Shush!' her mother cautioned. 'Don't talk about it to your Dad. He's that upset about it all. It's bringing back such memories, you see, love. He's been dreading the water level dropping so low that the old buildings will be exposed. It's a sacrilege to him.'

'I would have thought he would have liked to have seen it all again,' she said, suddenly ashamed of her excitement. Her mother looked sympathetic and shook her head sadly.

'He's had enough trouble trying to forget about the valley being flooded. He's always grieved for the old farm. I think if he has to see it all again it will break his heart.'

Her mother's words sent a chill into Martha's heart and she shivered, despite the warmth of the evening. Her father was like a rock in her life and she didn't like the idea of his heart being broken. 'It will rain soon, it's always raining in Yorkshire,' she said comfortingly, pulling her hair back into a pony tail. 'Then everything will be better. It's so hot tonight it might even thunder . . . '

But it didn't rain that night or any day or night for several weeks. After the conversation with her mother her visits to the valley became like a guilty secret. Each evening at dusk she walked down with the puppies and counted out the stones of the old road which had snaked down the hillside in earlier times and was now clearly visible.

So strong was her urge to see the lost valley that she also began rising early, as soon as dawn broke, and slipping down to the lake-side, anxious for the first sight of the buildings which she knew were just below the surface of the remaining water. These early trips, running through the dew drenched grass in the cool morning air, in a silence broken only by the sweet song of the skylarks, became a little oasis of peace in her life. A time when there was no heat, no questions which she didn't feel like answering, and no telephone which never rang for her.

The morning that the church appeared was misty: a white coiling heat haze which hung across the valley like a great rolling eiderdown. At first she couldn't get her bearings, the mist made the now familiar slopes an alien place. But then, looming under her feet she saw a black gnarled shape like an alligator and she instinctively took two steps back. Then, with a little laugh at her own foolishness, she saw that the object was an old tree root. Next, with a cry of excitement, she realised that there was mud under her sandals and not hard-baked mud. The mist shifted, and for a moment, she had a tantalising glimpse of stones and a broken arch . . . It was the ruins of the church — the church where her parents had married, where her brothers and sister had been baptised. The church which she had never seen.

It was then she became aware of the fact that she was not alone: someone else was standing at the edge of the water, another person who had been drawn here to watch this strange unveiling of the past. Martha turned, quite angry that this special moment she had been waiting for should be spoiled by an onlooker. A tall shape was coming through the mist and she said loudly and rather rudely: 'Do you realise you are trespassing?'

The person laughed: she knew then it was a man and this made her more irritated: 'What are you doing here?

This is private land,' she said again. At that moment the mist began to thin and the low rays of the morning sun broke through. The stranger was suddenly in front of her and illuminated in a ray of sun like a spot-light. Martha gasped and took a step back, for she experienced the oddest sensation. Before her she saw the height and form of a man, but the sudden shaft of light turned his hair to gold, and for a moment the artist in her was spellbound by the contrasts between his gleaming masculine vitality, the white enfolding mist and the dark wet earth beneath his feet.

She blinked and the ethereal beauty of the scene was gone. Before her stood a stranger, who like her wore rumpled shorts and shirt, as if he too had pulled on yesterday's clothes and dashed down here to check the water level. He pushed his hand through his hair, brushing off the droplets of water from the mist. His face was beaded with moisture, so that his light eyebrows and the gold stubble on his cheeks glistened.

When he spoke she found his voice was very deep and curiously gentle. 'I'm sorry if I startled you. I was so desperate to get a picture of the church I walked around the top of the lake. It was very remiss of me. My only excuse is that it is so early I assumed I wouldn't be caught.' He laughed again, the joke was obviously on him and Martha found the scowl on her face lifting slightly. 'Would you mind if I took a photograph of you, there with the tree stump, the sun is coming up behind you . . . ' He raised his camera, she knew at a glance it was not the kind of equipment which tourist and holiday makers carry, and said furiously:

'Wait! You're not from a newspaper, are you?'

'No, I'm not,' he said quietly and he lowered his camera and waited for a reply. Martha didn't answer and he said again, patiently: 'May I take your picture?'

'I suppose so,' she said ungraciously,

looking down at her feet suddenly as gawky as a school-girl. And before she could look up or smile, the camera whirled and clicked. 'I wasn't ready!' she protested.

The man laughed. 'That was how I wanted it! It will be a wonderful photo, the light is magical. I shall be here tonight, or as near as I can get to this spot without trespassing, because it's a full moon. If you want to see the photo I'll bring it along.'

'All the fields on this side of the valley belong to my family's farm and are private.' Her voice was firm: she didn't want to share the emerging village with anyone else, this was her special, secret place. 'You will be trespassing if you come to this side of the lake. The other side belongs to the Davies', they might not mind you traipsing over their land but my father objects to people trampling down his fences and leaving gates open.' To her surprise the man took little notice of her haughty tone but smiled kindly and said:

'I quite understand, but I think I can be trusted not to do either of those things. So I'll see you here at about ten o'clock, shall I?'

Martha frowned and began to walk off without answering, she felt out-manoeuvred and slightly foolish.

'Don't rush off, the sun will be up in a few moments and the mist is clearing. There will be lots to see,' he called after her.

With sudden unreasonable anger she turned on him. In her heart she knew that she was angry with herself, because she had been shouting her mouth off about trespassing and practically accused him of being the kind of person who leaves gates open and wrecks fences: one of the greatest insults which rural people can make to complete strangers! And he, in contrast to her truculence, had been unfailingly polite, almost wryly amused by her posturing, as if she were an irritable child who needed humouring.

'You may have all day but I

have a baby at home,' she said crossly. 'I haven't got time to stand around looking at old stones.' And, having snapped that out, she flounced off across the hard-baked earth. To her utter astonishment he called out cheerfully: 'Come at ten. It will be a cracking photo of you.'

Martha had no intention of going down to the lake at ten o'clock. She didn't feel that she had come off best in this strange confrontation and she hoped she would never see the man again. She was confused and slightly ashamed of her ill-temper. Weeks of hot weather and worry had turned her into a shrew. Grinning ruefully at the memory of her outburst she resolved to be more sunny natured and to get out more. It seemed ages since she had spoken to anyone but the postman and her parents. And then when she did meet someone new she was rude to them! But the day did not turn out as she expected.

'There's a letter for you, love,' her

mother said when she returned to the house. 'From London,' she added with an anxious frown.

There had been no word from Toby during the weeks she had been at the farm, not a letter, note or phone call. Many, many times she had found herself at the phone, sometimes with the receiver in her hand, sometimes with a finger raised ready to punch out the number. But something stopped her, some complex emotion which was a mixture of pain, pride and fear. Now she reached for the letter with a hand which was not quite steady and the sight of Toby's bold artistic writing almost took her breath away. He had struck out their London address and scribbled the address of the farm in vivid purple felt-tip. Just for a moment she could see him so clearly; sitting in his studio, pushing his dark hair from his forehead as he reached into the chipped mug which held his pens and snatching up the first which came to hand.

The logo on the letter told her that it came from their mortgage company, but even so she was unprepared for the contents. They informed her that their mortgage had not been paid.

'Everything all right?' Her mother's worried voice brought her out of the daze she was in.

'Nothing which can't be sorted out,' Martha said lightly. Now was the time to tell her mother everything, but something stopped her. It seemed impossible to put into words the sense of betrayal she was experiencing.

All day she was preoccupied with her worries and didn't even remember the man as she made her way down to the lake in the cool of the evening. Her footsteps were slow and she was so deep in thought that when the dogs began to bark she gave a little startled cry. Looking up she could see him standing nonchalantly, watching the moon rising over the hillside while the pups, Ross and Dolly jumped up at him. He turned and waved as she made her way over to him. By the time she arrived he had soothed and calmed the dogs and they lay panting at his feet for all the world as if they belonged to him.

Martha laughed and said with a touch of bitterness: 'I see you have a way with dogs.'

'So it would appear, these two seem to like me . . . ' There was the same amused tone he had used with her that morning, as if everything, including himself, was worth laughing at. 'What are their names?'

'Ross and Dolly.'

'I'm Jez, by the way,' he said. There was a pause, but she didn't tell him her own name, she didn't feel in the mood to be friendly. Her good resolutions from the morning had vanished. She wished he would go away and leave her alone in her misery.

'Are you a professional photographer?' she asked reluctantly.

'Yes, I am,' he said with a grin. 'Although sometimes I think it's a daft

28

way to make a living. But then I find a topic which really stirs me and I'm off again. Maybe one day I'll settle down with a nice little photographic shop somewhere . . . ' He was laughing aloud now. 'My next trip is to the Himalayas. I'm researching a feature on Sherpas, but I may be able to photograph a snow-leopard as well, if I'm lucky.'

'Settling down isn't all it's cracked up to be. I should stick to travelling and forget about the shop,' she said ruefully. Moving across to the edge of the lake she found a large stone and sat down. She hoped he might take the hint and leave but he followed her over and finding a similar stone sat down. Ross and Dolly lay panting between them.

'That is a very bitter remark for someone so young,' he said softly. 'Has life treated you badly?'

'Yes and no . . . ' surprisingly she tried to answer him truthfully. 'I have a beautiful baby boy who is an absolute blessing, *but* . . . '

There was silence between them, the dogs rose and moved off, nosing amongst the bushes. The only sound was their snuffling breath and the lonely call of a night jar. In the sky above them the moon rose like a gigantic silver salver set upon an enormous tablecloth of midnight-blue velvet.

'Tell me about the *but* . . . ' he suggested gently.

Martha shrugged but then unexpectedly found herself talking in a rush. 'Do you know if the valley hadn't been flooded I would have lived at Northend Village because Bridge End Farm, next to the river, belonged to my family.'

'But you never saw it,' he said softly.

'No . . . the valley was flooded the year I was born. It was a bad year for my family. They lost a great deal; all their best land which they had farmed for generations, their home, their village, their church. I don't think my Dad has ever got over it.' There was silence. Martha glanced at the man, he was looking straight ahead across the narrow strait of water which now separated the hillsides, he seemed preoccupied as if he was only half listening to her. His aloofness gave her confidence. Suddenly it was like talking to herself and not confiding in a stranger. And now she had started the words slid away from her as it they had a life of their own.

'My parents have never had a holiday, never bought a new car. My dad works seven days a week from dawn to dusk and still can't make ends meet. I used to think it was the price you paid for running your own farm, but it isn't like that for everyone.'

'No . . . ' he agreed. 'It isn't.'

Suddenly, unexpectedly, she found she was crying silently, tears which she had not shed before filled her eyes and trickled down her cheeks. Brushing them hastily away she was glad of the darkness and the man's apparent lack of interest.

'When I got married Mam and Dad produced money they had been saving all their life for me. They did the same for my brothers and sister. A fare to New Zealand for Tom. Shares in a co-operative dairy in Canada for Eddie. A setting-up-home sum for Ruth. And the same for me . . . not a lot of money, but enough, with my savings, to use as a deposit for a house when I got married.'

'They sound like wonderful parents: you are very lucky,' his voice was low and caring.

'All those years they went without and scraped along, just so we could have a good start. I don't know how to tell them . . . ' Her voice broke and she buried her face in her hands. The tears had turned into a torrent, there was no way she could hide them now. She felt a gentle hand on her shoulder and a crisp cotton handkerchief being pushed into her fingers. He didn't speak and she rattled on, not caring that her words were disjointed or that she wasn't really making sense. It was such a relief to finally talk to someone.

'They didn't try to persuade me not to marry Toby — it would probably have only made me more determined. But I knew they were fearful for me. I could see it in their eyes, in the guarded way they spoke about him. But they still gave me the money . . . '

'Why don't you start at the beginning, I want to help you.'

'But you're a stranger . . . ' she said, bemused to suddenly find herself, sitting under the stars with this man, and talking of matters she had not dared to reveal to anyone else.

'Sometimes it's easier to talk about things to someone you don't know. They don't carry any emotional baggage for you. That is why people go to therapists and psychiatrists,' he said lightly.

'I got married when I was at art college, Toby was much more talented than me so when we graduated I got a teaching job and he pursued his career as a painter.'

'How very convenient for him to have a beautiful wife to keep him from starving in a garret,' the man said wryly.

'Yes, and it was Mam and Dad's money and my earnings which paid for the house we bought. Toby's earnings were too erratic to pay for anything but luxuries. Things were fine, his career was going well but then I got pregnant. He went mad. He was furious and even suggested . . . ' Her voice faltered, unable to frame the words which would have meant that her darling Luke would never have been born.

'I understand. What happened then?'

'Well, we were still living under the same roof, but things were pretty terrible between us. But I was too proud and pig-headed to admit I had made a mistake. I suppose I didn't want to admit to myself it was over so

I carried on paying the mortgage and the bills from my savings. Toby wanted me to go back to work full-time and I wanted to work part-time so I could spend time with Luke.'

'So you left and came home . . . '

'It wasn't just that . . . One day I found some bills and receipts in Toby's jacket pocket. I realized my suspicions that he was having an affair were right and while he was bullying me about leaving my baby and going back to work he was spending money on another woman. I left that night, I haven't spoken to him since. But now . . . well he's refused to pay the mortgage. My savings are nearly gone . . . If I'm not careful the house will be repossessed and I will have lost everything. I can't bear to think of Mam and Dad scrimping and saving for all those years to give me a good start in life and I've wasted it all . . . '

Twisting his hanky into a ball with nervous fingers, she stared into the darkness, too hurt to say more. He watched her intently, his face pale and finely etched in the moon-light.

'You need some practical help. I've got a friend, a lawyer in Skipton, she deals with cases like this all the time. I know she'll help.' He drew a notebook and pen from his camera bag and jotted down a name and phone number. 'Phone her tomorrow. Promise?'

'Promise . . . ' she said shyly. 'Thank you for listening. I'd better get home, and let you get on with your photographs.'

'I think I've missed the best of the evening — the cloud is thickening. If it is all right for me to trespass for another evening I'd like to come tomorrow.'

'Okay,' she said, turning to leave and whistling for the dogs.

'Wait a minute. I haven't given you the photograph I took this morning. It's brilliant.' He handed her a print and illuminated it with a small flash-light.

'Oh heavens . . . ' she said with dismay. 'I look like a wild woman or a troll. I'd jumped out of bed and hadn't brushed my hair.' Then, remembering her manners she said more politely. 'Thank you anyway. It will be lovely to have a momento of the day the church appeared.'

As she began to move away the man's voice stopped her again. 'You still haven't told me your name,' he called softly. She glanced back quickly. His eyes were shadowed. The moon had disappeared behind a cloud. As she answered her voice sounded very small in the sudden darkness.

'Martha . . . my name is Martha. Good-bye,' she added rather formally.

'Goodbye, Martha,' he said with the same seriousness. And she was convinced suddenly that they would never meet again; and she wondered if, when he was in Nepal, he would ever think of this strange night of moonlight and confidences. She doubted it, and she didn't know if she was glad or sorry for that. Certainly she would never forget this evening when she had finally come to terms with what had been happening to her. It was as if she had awoken from a dream-like state which stopped her from reacting to events: and it was this meeting with a stranger which had woken her up.

As she walked briskly up the hill with the dogs she felt a new kind of strength filling her. Once she had loved Toby and been frightened she would lose him. Then she had ceased to love him but had still been frightened of losing him. Finally, now, tonight, she had admitted to another person how badly she had been hurt. Deep inside she knew that now she had faced up to losing Toby she could start to fight him . . . and win.

# 2

Martha phoned the firm of solicitors early the next morning and asked for the name on the piece of paper — Susanna Reed. At first she was nervous, her heart trembling and her forehead clammy, but the cheerful voice at the other end of the line soon put her at ease.

'Hi, Martha. Jez told me you might phone today. Look, I'm really busy but if you could get over here at noon I could see you and start the ball rolling. Jez says things are getting pretty difficult for you so we don't want to waste any time.'

'Thank you, it's very good of you to see me so quickly . . . '

'Oh, that's okay. Jez is an old friend and I'm pleased to help. And don't worry about bills,' the other woman said softly, as if reading her mind.

'There won't be any until I get you a settlement. Providing that is what you want . . . '

'I'm taking Luke into Skipton. I need to buy him some new clothes, he's grown out of everything.' Martha announced when she and Mam were having coffee.

'Oh, don't trail all the way into Skipton in this heat. Go into Harrogate,' Mam suggested.

'There's so little water in the valley it's almost possible to walk to Skipton. You can see the church down there now, Mam.'

As Martha spoke her mother shook her head as if the words were an irritation, like a wasp flying too close to her face: 'Pray that it rains soon then, our Martha,' her mother said sorrowfully. 'Your father saw the church flooded you know,' she confided, her voice low. 'The water authority thought that the water might leak away so they did a trial flood — just enough water to cover the bottom of the valley. Your

40

Dad was cutting trees in the meadow next to the churchyard when they let the first water in. He saw it come creeping over the graves and then dribbling in over the church steps, filling up the crypt and covering the tiles on the floor . . . ' Her mother stopped, her eyes pained. 'He came in and told me about it and there were tears in his eyes and he's never mentioned it again from that day to this. The whole business was hard for your Dad: it was like they cut away part of him when they took away the valley.'

Martha shivered at the memory of the blackened stones and the forlorn muddy ruins of the church. 'It's better that he doesn't see it. It does look sad . . . neglected and forgotten.'

'I wish it was forgotten.' Her mother said emphatically. 'Your father has never forgiven the Davies' for their part in it all. The old man died quite recently and I went to the church with some flowers to pay my respects: they were our neighbours for years, you know, but your Dad wouldn't come. All that resentment is still festering in him and doesn't do him any good. You can't turn the clock back. They say the son who had inherited the farm is going to sell up. And it will be a good job if he does, then there will be no more Davies' in the neighbourhood.'

Martha frowned, puzzled. 'But we never see them. I wouldn't know a Davies if I fell over one. Why does it matter?'

'I don't know why it matters but it does. They live over there in their big fine house with their pedigree herds. You can't open a Yorkshire Show result without the name jumping out at you: the old man used to win everything. Well, it just rubs salt into the wound for your Dad. They did so well out of the flooding of the valley and we did so badly. Things have never gone right for your Dad since we left the old farm. We've always bought the wrong animals, made the wrong investments. The BSE business has just about finished us off . . . '

Martha bit her lip. 'I'm sorry Mam. I won't mention it again. It's got to rain soon, surely?'

But as she drove away from the house the sky was an intense, cloudless blue and the sun a merciless golden globe. Rain didn't look likely today, if anything it was hotter than ever. Skipton was as she had never seen it before: vivid and bright, like a continental town, with people in colourful shorts and T-shirts; and the grey-stone buildings, which were more used to rain and mist than endless sunshine, were shimmering in the heat.

The offices of Reed, Browne and Holmes were tucked away behind the market square. Inside fans blew cool air and she was soon settled comfortably in Susanna Reed's office with a glass of iced tea. Luke slept in her arms, loosely wrapped in a cotton blanket. 'Isn't he gorgeous?' Susanna said, looking down at the baby's sleeping face and touching his silky dark hair with a cautious finger. 'Will he wake up soon?'

'Yes. I've got a drink ready in my bag and his lunch. The heat has worn him out. I thought it was hot up at the farm but it's worse down here in town.'

'You said on the phone that you want a divorce. But because of your age and the fact that you have such a young baby I feel I should urge you to try conciliation before you decide anything.' Susanna said gently, her eyes still on the sleeping child.

Martha looked at the slim elegant woman perched on the desk in front of her and shook her head slowly. 'I'm sorry. I know it ought to be possible, but it isn't. Toby lied, deceived and bullied me. He has completely destroyed my trust and I can't love someone I can't trust.'

'Having a child is often a testing time in a relationship,' Susanna said quietly, then, startled by the look in Martha's eyes, she added quickly: 'Or so people tell me. I'm sorry: it must seem to you that people who have no idea of what you have been through think they know what's best for you, and that can seem very arrogant. Forgive me. I've never been married, deceived or had a child so you tell me what it's like.'

Slowly, haltingly, holding the child close to her as she spoke, Martha told the whole sorry tale. Finally she finished by explaining that during the weeks she had been at the farm Toby had not contacted her once to enquire about the baby, Susanna shook her head sorrowfully. 'I'll start divorce proceedings for you. I just need some financial and background details.'

Just as they were finishing the phone rang. 'Someone's here to take you to lunch,' Susanna said with a smile, and, as she replaced the receiver, Jez walked in to the office. He kissed Susanna on the cheek and unexpectedly Martha found herself blushing at the thought that he might greet her in the same manner but he merely peered at the baby and said: 'Will you have time to eat before he wakes up?' At that moment Luke's eyes and mouth flew open and he gave his very best fog-horn wail for food. Jez burst out laughing and picked up her baby holdall. 'I thought we could have a bite to eat across the road. I've asked for a quiet table in an alcove. By the sound of him he's ready for his lunch.'

The hotel restaurant was nearly empty and wonderfully cool. The crisp white cloths on the table and the dark wood panelling was very soothing. Jez ordered a bottle of low-alcohol wine and asked for a bowl of boiling water to heat up the baby's bottle and food.

While Luke was sucking happily on his bottle, she looked across at Jez, who was stirring pureed vegetables for the child, and said with a smile: 'You appear to be a bit of an expert on babies.' Really she wanted to ask him if he was married and had children of his own but for some reason the question would not come out.

'I've got lots of nephews and nieces — my sisters have nine children between them. I've had plenty of practise.' He handed over the baby dish. 'I think it's warm enough. If I read the menu aloud would you like to choose your lunch? If we have a salad we can take it in turns to eat.'

Unexpected tears prickled the back of her eyes and she concentrated hard on spooning the food into Luke's mouth. She had never been out with the child before or shared the tasks of looking after him with anyone apart from her mother and father. Toby had ignored them both while they were in London and being in the restaurant with Jez suddenly gave her an insight into what it would be like to have a caring husband — and it hurt.

'Are you okay?' he asked, his voice concerned. 'I'm sorry if I hijacked you. I wanted to see you . . . I didn't realise you might not feel like being sociable after going over everything with Suzanna.'

'Oh, it's not that . . . ' she said, her chin trembling as she spoke. 'It's just you're being so kind.' She placed the empty dish on the table and held Luke up to hide her face.

'Here, let me be really kind and hold him over my shoulder. If my memory serves me well it's now they dribble out all the bits they didn't really want.' Jez said, placing a serviette over his back with a flourish like a conjurer. She found herself handing over the baby, laughing through her tears.

'I should like to photograph you like that,' Jez said, expertly rubbing the baby's back and smiled across at her: 'Sunshine and rain . . . ' For a moment there was a pause and their eyes met, then he continued lightly: 'My favourite kind of weather. I like rain, especially at Throstlegill when you see the clouds moving up the valley over the lake.'

'Yes, Mam always checks the valley from the sitting-room window before she hangs any washing out. If the sky is stormy we generally have about half an hour before it starts pouring. You see the clouds rolling up like an approaching army. I wish it would rain now . . . ' she added, rather forlornly.

'It's going to cause you real problems when the valley finally dries up and the whole village is exposed.' Jez said with a frown, his voice concerned. 'And it's bound to happen — there's no rain forecast for weeks.'

'My father is going to be very upset . . . '

'I imagine he will be.' Jez said grimly. 'And there will be problems with people visiting the valley — there's bound to be a lot of interest. The best thing your father could do is to turn one of his fields into a car-park and charge them for parking. Then he should mark out a footpath down to the old village. It might contain the problem. If not he will have cars parked everywhere, blocking his access, and people walking all over the fields.'

Martha stared at him horrified. 'He

won't do that! He runs the farm single handed with Mam and he doesn't have time to organize car parks or anything like that. And he'd hate people traipsing over his land. They'd never stay on the path and they'd drop litter. He'd go mad . . . '

'When the valley is dry it is bound to happen. It would be better really to meet the problem head-on.'

'Yes, you are right, I will try to talk to him. It's just that he's been so short-tempered since the drought started, not like himself at all.'

'Times are hard for farmers,' Jez said. Their food had arrived and he added: 'You eat your lunch, and don't hurry. I'm fine with this little lad.'

'How do you know so much about farming?' she asked curiously.

'My sisters are all married to farmers and I come from a farming family.'

'Most sons of farmers carry on with the tradition. Didn't the life appeal to you?'

'No . . . by the time I was born

50

my parents marriage was in trouble, and my mother spent all her time grumbling about the loneliness and hard-work. Then, when I was twelve, she left us and went to live in America. Ridiculously I blamed my father and the farm for the fact that she had abandoned us. My father and I never got on very well after that.'

'That must have been hard for you,' Martha said softly, recalling his comments the previous evening about how lucky she was with her parents. 'You must have felt as if you had lost both of them.'

'Yes, that is just how I felt.' For a rare moment Jez was completely serious. Then he grinned. 'I rejected the farm and rural life completely. I even joined the hunt saboteurs. But the strangest part of it all is that my father died not long ago and left the farm and all the land to me. Frankly I don't know what to do with it.'

'It's not a life to go in for unless you are totally committed. It's such hard work you have to love it,' she said slowly.

'And were you drawn towards it?' he asked. 'As you ended up as an art teacher I would guess not.'

Laughing, she wrinkled up her nose and said: 'I love the farm and I pine for the countryside when I am in the city but I also love painting. I just wish I'd been better at it and able to follow a creative career.'

'Will you show me some of your work? How good are you?' he asked with a grin.

'The answer to the first question is yes, if you really are interested: the answer to the second question is not as good at Toby.'

'Is your husband Tobias DeLeon?' Jez asked, his eyes suddenly narrowing.

Martha closed her eyes for a second as if a sudden pain had streaked across her heart, then she nodded, and Jez said gently: 'Well, not many people are as talented as him. He must be just about the best of his generation.'

'Yes,' she said dryly. 'And it's not easy living with a genius . . . ' She finished the last of her salad and said with a satisfied sigh: 'That was wonderful. Please have yours now.' She held out her hands for the baby and Jez handed him over. 'He's been very good for you,' she added with a smile.

'I think small children and dogs always know if you like them, they still have a special bit of intuition which the rest of us have lost.' Jez said, reaching for the jar of mustard and then attacking his beef salad. She watched him eating with a smile. He talked while he ate, telling her about the assignments he had taken, the places he had visited and the time raced by. Eventually, as they sat over coffee, she looked at her watch and gave a little gasp.

'I didn't realise it was so late. I shall have to go. My mother will think I've been abducted by aliens.'

When they got back to her car

she was suddenly beset by shyness. 'Thank you for lunch and thank you for introducing me to Suzanna,' she said holding out her hand to him. They shook hands solemnly, like strangers or politicians, which, considering she had told him the most intimate details of her life, seemed pretty silly to her. But she craved some kind of contact with him and that official gesture seemed the only way to manage it.

Before he released her hand he said: 'Will you come to the valley tonight?'

'I don't know . . .' she said, her emotions in sudden turmoil.

'I'll be there at ten o'clock — try to make it . . .' he said and he was frowning, as if he wanted to say more, but she left quickly.

During the rest of the day she told herself that she would not go to the valley that evening. It was the realisation that she had felt happier during lunch with Jez than she had for years which frightened her. She was reminded of the battery hens which her mother had once bought out of pity at the market and then tried to acclimatise to being free rangers. The poor things had huddled in corners, refusing to perch or peck like normal birds, unable to appreciate their new-found freedom. That was how she felt — scared of the outside world. Being with Jez had been like stepping from night into daylight and seeing a long vista of endless possibilities: a whole landscape of experiences and feelings which she had been deprived of for so long. But the glimpse she been offered had made her fearful. She told herself firmly that at the moment all she needed was to keep her eyes on the ground and sort out her problems.

'I will not go this evening,' she vowed. Biting at her lip she reminded herself that Jez was a nomad who rarely stayed long in one place, so it would be second nature to him to make friends quickly. Soon he would be leaving and then there would be other people to fill his mind, fellow travellers with tales to tell, people with problems at airports who would respond to a sympathetic face — as she had done. She was nothing special to him. Whereas he had become special to her and it was foolish for her to try to hide that fact from herself. And so she deliberately made herself busy and refused to look at the clock, determined that she would not go down to the valley.

Just as the ten o'clock news programme finished her mother said: 'Aren't you going to take those puppies for a little walk, Martha? They're whining.'

'You've taken them every other evening and got them into the habit now . . . ' her father added a little irritably, looking up from his accounts book with a frown.

Martha jumped guiltily: 'Yes, sorry, I will take them up the lane for a few moments. I won't be long . . . '

★ ★ ★

Jez watched the moon rising over the far hillside and took several photographs of the broken stones rising in sinister humps from the lake. The light was good: the moon casting long shadows on the dried earth of the valley and sliding silvery fingers across the water. But his heart wasn't in what he was doing and he realized that he was waiting for a foot fall, or for the sound of his name being called, to break the stillness of the night.

By ten thirty he realized that Martha was not coming and he walked down to the edge of the water and stared moodily at what remained of the lake. Soon, maybe by tomorrow even, every building would be revealed and the valley would be back to it's former shape: steeply sloping sides and a small meandering stream running next to an ancient village.

It was all much smaller than he remembered from his childhood; the hills surrounding the valley then had seemed a huge sweep of grass and the church which stood guard over the village a towering building. He could recall leaning over the bridge with his sisters, throwing sticks from one side and running across to watch them float out of the other in the speedy current.

As a child he had regularly visited the church with its cool red brick floor and pervading musty scent of damp hymn books and old flowers. He had always walked quickly through the graveyard with it's mossy leaning tombstones, some so old they had been wiped clean by the elements; because once, while playing hide and seek, he had run across the tempting green humps and overturned a flower urn, and his sisters had filled his head with stories of ghosts and spooks who would retaliate for having their peace disturbed.

Most clearly of all he could remember the day the valley was flooded. Until then the building of the reservoir had seemed an enormous adventure. The arrival of bull-dozers and construction teams at the far end of the valley had filled the whole of the long summer holidays with excitement as he watched the dam being built. But the momentous day when the waters had been let in had been an anti-climax. He had assumed that there would be a rushing roar and a great wall of water would gush into the valley. In his imagination he had seen people and animals scattering, taking to the hills at a run. But there had been a trial flooding and then a gradual filling up. How the family had laughed at his disappointment. 'You'll have to be patient, Jeremy. It will take time to turn into a lake, his father had said, while he had chafed at the delay in using the new boat his father had bought for the children. His disappointment had eased after the lake was established because it had become a great source of joy in their lives, there was the endless fun of sailing, fishing and watching the teeming bird life.

Now the lake was disappearing and

the emerging of the old village seemed to symbolise something in his life, but he didn't know what it was or how it fitted into the confusion he felt about his future. He just sensed that something momentous was about to happen to the valley and to the people who lived there.

He shook his head to try to dispel the strange fancies which filled his mind. It was then he heard barking and felt the weight of dogs running into his legs. Crouching down he stroked the sleek black and white heads, and allowed the puppies to lick his hand in greetings: 'Have you two come down on your own?' he asked, disappointed. They lay down at his feet, panting, and it was then that he saw a small figure scrambling down the hill side and he found himself smiling as he began to walk quickly to meet her.

'I thought you would be gone by now . . . ' she said artlessly and he laughed and reached for her hand.

'Come and see the water level. We're

nearly down to the bottom of the valley. The church is clear but full of mud. You can make out the chancel and the nave.' Her hand pulled away from him and he sensed her reluctance.

'I don't think I want to see it,' she said miserably.

'Okay,' he said. 'Let's walk for a bit. There is something else I want to show you.' For a while they walked in silence. Above the hillside the moon rose like a great silver disc, and in the distance an owl hooted. Nearer at hand a nightjar called with a mournful note and the air was fragrant with the scent of wild thyme.

They walked around the curve of the hillside until the house on the opposite side of the lake was in view. It was an old stone-built farm surrounded by barns and outbuildings. Too high up upon the hillside to have been affected by the flooding of the valley, the only change for the inhabitants after the deluge had been that, instead of looking down on Northend valley, the view from their windows was of a sheet of gleaming water.

There was a light in one of the upstairs rooms which shone out like a beacon over the valley. Jez stopped and pointed: 'I left my bedroom light on so we would be able to see it. Martha, that house, Beckwith Farm, is my home.' He was unprepared for her response, she recoiled from him as if he had hit her.

'No . . . ' she gasped, turning away from him.

'Martha, what is it?' He took hold of her shoulders and tried to turn her around to face him so that he could see her face, but she pulled away.

'You're Jeremy Davies. Why on earth did you tell me your name was Jez?' Her voice was icy. 'And why didn't you tell me who you were when I was telling you off for trespassing? I suppose you thought it was funny, letting the little farm girl make a fool of herself . . . ' There was no doubting the anger in her voice now. 'I would never have agreed to meet you again or had lunch with you . . . or anything . . . if I'd known you were a Davies . . . ' she ended. Then she turned, her auburn hair flying in a curtain behind her, as if to run away.

'Martha,' he said sternly. 'Wait and at least let me explain. You owe me that.'

She turned, her head bowed, waiting for him to speak.

'I told you my name was Jez because that is what everyone calls me and it is the name I use for my work. The name Jez Davies is printed on the back of the photograph I gave you. So you can't really accuse me of deliberately deceiving you.'

'That's not the point. You should have told me when we first met . . . ' she protested angrily. She turned her face away from him and he could see her lovely profile, the high forehead and the curve of her mouth clearly in the moonlight.

He sighed. This was proving harder

than he had imagined. 'I have to admit that I didn't tell you the first morning we met partly because you amused me. But also because I wanted you to like me for myself. I know there has been bad feelings between our families. I didn't want us to get involved with all that straight away. I thought now we are friends I could tell you and it wouldn't matter.'

'Not matter?' she asked aghast. 'You must be mad to think it wouldn't matter. My father is still paying the price of your father's treachery. He is devastated by the village coming back and the last thing in the world he would want is us being friends. Anyway, I'm not in the position to be friends with anyone at the moment. I've got a divorce to sort out and a baby to look after.' He could hear the shadow of a tear in her voice, a huskiness which twisted at his heart.

'Martha,' he pulled her into his arms. The top of her head came up to the second to top button on his shirt. He rested his face on the silken softness of her hair and tightened his hold on her. Through the thin material he could feel the heat of her face, and could almost imagine the sigh of her breath on his skin.

'Martha. I know my father was in the wrong. He knew it too. But we don't have to fight that old battle all over again, surely?'

'Oh, we'll find a new battle, shall we?' she said, pulling away from him, her face raising defiantly to his. 'You deceived me, Jez. You made a fool of me as well, letting me rattle on about shutting gates and such like.' He could hear from her voice that she was getting more angry and he steeled himself for an onslaught. 'I've had enough of being deceived and talked down to,' she added bitterly. 'Years and years of it. I don't want it anymore. I don't want anything to do with people I can't trust. I just hope you sell your farm quickly and I never see you again.'

She pulled right away from him then and the feeling of her small body in his arms was just a fleeting memory.

'I'm sorry you feel like this about it.' He was deliberately cool to hide how hurt he was by her outburst. 'I thought we could be friends.'

'Well, you thought wrong, didn't you?' she snapped. 'Anyway there's no point. You'll be off on your travels in a few days . . . The valley and me, well we've just been a distraction for you, haven't we?' She was really angry now. Her red hair should have warned him that she would have a temper. He pushed his hand through his hair, at a loss to know how to reply to her accusations.

She was turning now, whistling for the dogs, walking as quickly as she could away from him. 'Martha,' he called. 'If I said I was sorry would it help at all?'

Shaking her head she didn't reply. Something about the despairing set of her shoulders made him think she might be crying. A clutch of emotions, protectiveness, sorrow and anger fought within him for a moment; then, with a whispered curse, he ran after her, covering the distance in a couple of seconds. He spun her around and clasped her close and she was so startled that for a moment she was as relaxed as a child in his arms. A small shuddering sob ran through her. 'Martha,' he whispered. 'Please don't let us fight.' Then he kissed her very slowly, letting his mouth cover hers gently. He could taste the salt from her tears on her lips. Slowly, very slowly, she kissed him back and for many moments they stood clasping each other.

Finally she drew back with a shudder. 'We shouldn't have done that,' she whispered. 'Why did you do it? I didn't want to kiss you.'

'Yes you did,' he said softly, reaching for her and covering her mouth again. 'We both did. You can't choose these things, Martha. Sometimes they just happen. Now, tell me you forgive me. We can't part with all this acrimony and fighting. It's just pathetic to quarrel after all the fun and laughter we've had together . . . '

'I forgive you,' she said. 'But I just hope I never see you again. And, if I have anything to do with it, I won't!' And with that stinging retort she took to her heels. He watched her running up the hill with the dogs racing and barking behind her. He would try to be content with the fact that she had said she had forgiven him — but in his heart he knew it wasn't enough.

For the first time since he had been living alone at Beckwith Farm the house seemed lonely when he returned. The phone was ringing with an insistent bleep and he frowned as he picked up the receiver.

'Jez? I've been ringing for the last two hours. Where on earth have you been?' It was Heather, the eldest of his sisters.

'Walking . . . '

'Tut, it's nearly midnight. I was worried I might have missed you. Lydia says you are off to Nepal any day now.'

'I'm not going. I phoned my agent this morning.'

'Not going?' Heather sounded scandalised. 'Why ever not?'

'Because there are lots of young, keen, hungry photographers out there queuing up to work and I don't feel like going. There are things I want to sort out here, the farm, what I'm going to do with it, and what I'm doing with my life.'

'Is something the matter?' Heather asked.

'Not really. I just need time to think. I've been travelling non-stop for eight years now, rushing from one assignment to another, terrified to let up in case someone else got the pictures before me, maybe I'm burned out.'

Heather laughed: 'Lydia says you're seeing a girl, has that got anything to do with your sudden desire to stick around here? I would have thought it would be deadly dull after all your globe-trotting.'

'What makes Lydia think I've got a girlfriend?' he asked quietly.

'You were seen at Talbots by a friend of Lyd's — she thought it looked like a romance. You know how everyone talks. Who is she?'

'I took Martha Hetherington out for lunch. I'm surprised there wasn't a piece in the local paper about it,' he replied bitterly.

'Well!' Heather said. 'You have surprised me! A Hetherington having lunch with a Davies. Are you sure she didn't try to poison you?'

'No,' he said wearily. 'She didn't realise who I was, that was why she agreed to have lunch with me. There's no romance, nothing like that. Suzanna was helping her with her divorce that's how I met her. Tell the snoops to leave it alone, please Heather.'

'You sound awfully fed up. You'll

die from boredom if you stay there, you know.'

'My life is not at all boring, Heather. I rather wish it was. Please stop talking to me as if I were still six years old. I'm fine. I'll come over and see you soon.'

Jez showered and went to bed but could not sleep. Eventually he rose and padded down to the cellar where he had made himself a darkroom. The night was cool and very quiet. He normally liked to play music when he worked but that night he worked in silence, developing and enlarging photographs.

At last his watch told him that dawn would be breaking and he went up to the kitchen and made coffee, he drank it thick and bitter-black to compensate for his sleepless night, then he jogged down to the side of the lake nearest to the Hetherington's farm. He hung around for a while, but Martha didn't come down the hillside.

Much as he wanted to see her, he

was glad in a way that she didn't come: because the moment which he had both longed for and feared had arrived. The valley was dry — there was no water left apart from a trickling streamlet under the ruins of the bridge — and everything was there to be seen: old stone pig-sties and byres and the crumbling walls of farmhouse and barns. Bridge End Farm, home to the Hetheringtons for so long, had finally come back to them. And a sorry sight it was, the walls so black and thick with mud it was impossible to believe that people had once lived there. The valley had an atmosphere of strange unreality which environments take on after disaster: a place out of time with itself and the rest of the world. With a sigh, and a sad shake of his head, he turned away from the raw nakedness of the destruction and made his way home.

# 3

Martha had spent weeks watching the water disappearing at Throstlegill reservoir and waited with fear and trepidation for the day it vanished completely; but after her fraught meeting with Jez she didn't go down to the valley for two days, and so missed the sight of the farm and bridge appearing. Instead she heard the news on the local radio station as she and Mam were drinking coffee in the kitchen.

'You'll have to make Dad understand what this means,' she said desperately to her mother. 'People will be arriving in droves to look at the village.'

'But there's nothing to see,' her mother replied in despair. 'It was our home and we don't want to look at it. Why should other folks bother?'

Martha shook her head. 'I don't know, but they will come. And Dad will have to accept it. If I go and find him, will you please look after Luke? Where will Dad be at this time in the morning?'

Just then the telephone phone rang. Her mother answered it: 'It's a man, asking for you, Martha. But it's not Toby,' she added quickly.

Martha was furious with herself as she took the receiver because her hand was not quite steady. 'Yes,' she said curtly.

'Martha? It's Jez.'

'Yes,' she said again, even more stiffly. 'What do you want?' Was it her imagination or did he sigh a little at her unfriendly tone?

'Have you seen the Yorkshire Post this morning?' he asked quietly.

'No.' Even before the words were out she knew what he was going to say and her mouth was dry as she listened.

'There is a big aerial photo of the valley on the front page, there's no water left. It's all there to be seen, the farm, the bridge, the church. The visitors will start straight away.'

'Yes. Thank you for ringing,' she said and was ready to hang up but he said her name, his voice low but determined.

'Martha, before you go. Promise me that if you need any help you'll remember I'm here.'

'I don't think . . . ' she began.

'Don't say no,' he said quietly. 'Just tell me you'll call if you're in trouble.'

She opened her mouth to say 'no' but instead 'yes' came out and that seemed to satisfy him. 'Goodbye Martha,' he said quietly and the phone went dead.

'Who was that?' her mother asked curiously, but she didn't have time to answer because the back door opened with a thud and her father stood there breathing erratically as if he had been running: his face was a horrible grey colour and his right arm was hanging awkwardly. Martha and her mother rushed forward. Martha helped him into a chair while her mother reached into the drawer for a clean table cloth.

'My arm's broken, I heard it go . . . ' her father breathed and Martha nodded in agreement as she gently made a sling and supported the arm as best she could.

'I'll drive Dad down to the hospital,' she said, looking at her mother's shocked ashen face. 'You keep an eye on Luke for me, Mam.'

Martha drove as carefully as she could down the rough road which led from the house to the main highway, silently cursing the bank manager who had never lent them enough money to get the lane resurfaced and the drought which had turned the puddlepits into craters. For a while her father didn't speak but when he did his voice was a kind of hoarse whisper: 'I'll not be able to work with a pot on my arm . . . this is the end for us . . . '

'It will be all right, Dad. Don't worry about that now. You've got me at home. I'll do the milking and what ever needs to be done. At least the lambing is over,' Martha said calmly.

'How did it happen?'

'I was up in the ten acre when I heard voices. When I came down I could see a group of people traipsing straight across the fields with the gates swinging open. I ran and tried to jump the wall. Stupid old fool that I am. Used to be able to do it in my young days but not anymore.' Despite his pain her father managed a rueful smile. 'Any road I managed to pick myself up and get over to the gate in the yarrow field before the tup got out. He'd have charged them all and they'd have been down to the bottom of the valley sooner than they'd have expected. Tup'll have to be put in the barn straightaway. It's not safe having him out with daft folk leaving gates open . . . ' he added bitterly.

'The valley is dry, Dad. They've come to look at the old village. It's front page news, it was even on the radio.'

Her father shook his head in disbelief. 'Goodness knows why they want to look at those muddy old ruins . . . '

'Anyway, don't you worry about it.' Martha soothed, heaving a sigh of relief as they pulled onto the main road and she could put her foot down and get up some speed. 'I'll put up some notices and get it sorted out. Just you relax.'

It was only after they had arrived at the hospital and two kindly nurses had taken charge that shock set in and Martha began shaking like a leaf in a gale. Despite this she could not sit still, but paced the corridor waiting for someone to tell her something. At one o'clock she realized she should have some lunch even though she wasn't hungry, so she bought a sandwich and a chocolate bar from the WRVS and forced herself to eat, although it was like swallowing sawdust.

Finally, when her nerves felt ragged with waiting and worrying, a young doctor came out to talk to her: 'We've set your father's arm. It's a straightforward fracture and nothing to get too worried about, although these type of injuries do take longer to heal in older people. What I am more worried about is your father's general health.' He looked sympathetic as Martha blurted out:

'But Dad is never ill. He's never had a day in bed, or a cold, or anything . . . '

'The doctor smiled kindly as he said: 'That, I'm sure, is partly due to his good constitution and iron willpower. But his blood pressure is very high and he seems very stressed, very anxious about the farm. I've told him that no one is indispensable but he doesn't seem to believe me.'

'He's had a lot of worry recently. The BSE crisis has hit him hard and so had the new milk quotas. Life isn't easy for small mixed farms these days.' Martha said miserably.

'I'm sure they're not. What he really needs is a rest. A real rest. Somewhere away from the farm and his worries. He won't be able to use the arm for several weeks anyway and it is vital that he doesn't try to. Medication can be used to control his blood pressure but he does need to rest. He's not getting any younger . . . '

Martha stared up at the doctor, dumb with worry and misery. He patted her arm encouragingly and said: 'You can go in and see him now. He's been asking for you. But try not to worry him if you can help it. I've given him a sedative and we'll keep him in overnight.'

Her father was in a small side room, tucked under a neatly folded sheet. Although he appeared to be nearly asleep he reached out and took hold of her hand. 'We're finished, lass,' he said miserably.

'No we're not,' Martha said firmly. 'I've had plenty of time to think things over and I've decided I'm going to run the farm for you.'

'You're nowt but a slip of a lass . . . ' her father demurred. 'You might be able to keep up with the milking and feeding for a few days but the doctor says it'll be weeks before I can use this arm.'

'Well, by then I'll be used to hard work and really good at it, now stop worrying,' she said, taking hold of his uninjured hand and pressing it between both of hers.

'You're a good lass, Martha,' he said gently as his eyes closed and she stayed holding his hand until he was fast asleep. Then, with a heavy heart, she made her way back to the car and drove home.

'I've just walked the baby up the lane,' her mother said when Martha arrived back at the farmhouse. 'And you would not believe it, there are at least a dozen cars parked at the side of the road and about twenty people walking straight across down the valley through the fields. You're father will go mad when he sees it . . . ' she added gloomily.

'He won't have to see it,' Martha said decisively. 'I phoned Ruth she's

81

driving down this afternoon and she's going to take him back to Scotland for a couple of weeks. He'll never rest if he comes home. Could you give Luke his lunch, please Mam? I've got work to do. The first thing I'm going to do is to open up the twelve acre field, make a sign saying CAR PARK and an honesty box for people to put fifty pence in. At least it might stop them from blocking the road. Then I'm going to mark out a footpath and put some old feed bins out for litter. I'm going to get our tourist attraction organized!'

The sun was at it's hottest while she was working and the flies were a nuisance but it was gratifying that several people came in, parked, left their money and complimented her on the footpath and litter bins. Cheerfully checking the time Martha decided to look over the sheep which were grazing the top moor before starting the evening milking.

'Will you have a cup of tea, love?'

Her mother asked anxiously when she popped into the kitchen to check on Luke.

'I haven't time,' Martha said, downing a couple of glasses of water and grabbing a biscuit from the tin. 'I'll have one when I get back.'

Martha took her father's working crook with the carved horn handle from the back porch and called for Smiley, her father's sheep dog, to follow her. To her astonishment Smiley refused to move from his kennel.

'Come on, Smiley,' she said gently going over and patting his head. 'I know it's hot and your dad isn't here, but I need some help.'

Smiley raised his head and looked at her, sniffing the air. Then, finding that she was not the person he wanted, he put his head on his paws and closed his eyes. Martha sighed with a mixture of pity and exasperation. 'Come on, old fellow, I need a hand . . . or a paw. I can't round the sheep up on my own. Come on,' she added more sternly taking hold of his collar.

Reluctantly, his tail between his legs, his chin nearly touching the ground, he followed her over to the Land Rover but when she opened the door and said: 'Hup, good dog,' he sidled back to his kennel and sat down. Then, with a small whine, he returned to his former position, waiting for the sight and sound of his master.

With a mutter of dismay Martha realized Smiley would not work for her and, opening the puppy pen, she called out with what she hoped was a note of authority in her voice: 'Dolly, Ross. Time for work.'

Martha knew there was something wrong as soon as she drove up the lane, but her mind was full of the job in hand, and it took a few moments for her mind to register what was happening. At first she thought the lack of visibility was a summer heat haze swinging in a dusky curtain down from the top moor: then the acrid smell told her that the soft greyness in the air was smoke and a wave of panic engulfed her.

The puppies sat in subdued silence beside her as she revved the engine and began the long steep ascent to the top of the hillside where the sheep grazed. Swinging across the cattle grid which kept the animals on the moor a vicious patchwork of black soot, orange flames and white-bleached grass met her eyes — the moor was on fire.

The wind, like a capricious child, suddenly changed directions: she saw the flames leap back towards her and the Land Rover was suddenly engulfed in a cloud of smoke. When it cleared she could see a line of flames running across the moor, flickering high into the sky when it reached a tussock of heather and disappearing for a moment when it plunged into a drainage ditch. It was like a living thing: a monster feeding on dry vegetation and dancing with pleasure at the destruction in its wake. As she sprang down from the Land Rover she heard the sound of the fire, a sinister menacing crackle. Mingling with it was the frantic bleating of the sheep.

Martha knew the sheep would be fleeing — they would be herding up behind the leader and running scared. The problem was there was nowhere for them to run, there was no escape from the moor. Eventually they would be trapped against the boundary wall and the flickering, gobbling monster would follow them.

With a sob she began heaving open the gate at the side of the cattle grid. Nettles and cow parsley had grown around it since it was last opened and it took all the strength in her body to move it. But she knew that there was only one chance for the flock and that was if she could herd them back past the fire and out through the gate.

Quickly making plans she opened a gate further down the hill which led into a secure field and blocked the road with the Land Rover. Then, running and yelling for the puppies to follow her, she was back in the smoke; running across the moor, trying to find the sheep.

The puppies didn't want to follow, their tails were low and their eyes agonised but they came with her and she soon spotted the flock, they had gathered on the crag, the high ground, and looked set to stay there. She knew that eventually the wicked little wind which puffed and snorted the smoke into her eyes would move around the crag and take the flames with it: then the flock would be surrounded. Her heart was pounding in her chest but she ran on until she felt she was close enough to send the dogs in.

Her father made rounding up sheep look easy. He and Smiley worked with a peculiar grace and economy of commands and movement, like the steps of some dignified dance. Not so Dolly and Ross. They were valiant in following Martha, and, despite their youth, they crouched and ran when she whistled and herded to the right and left according to her commands: but the smoke made them nervous so they ran too fast and nipped at the stragglers, this onslaught and the smoke so terrified the sheep that rounding them up became like a wild-west rodeo with whirling animals and thudding hooves.

After a frantic twenty minutes she realized that the flock was too large for her to move all together. The dogs were losing the animals and upsetting them. Her only hope was to split it up into smaller groups and get a few at a time down the hill and through the gate.

At her first attempt only fifteen sheep were separated from the main group and herded out across the moor, and all the time the flames were moving closer. Wiping sweat and ash from her eyes she turned again, whistling for the dogs, even if it took all day she would try to save as many sheep as possible.

When she heard the sound of a engine and saw her Land Rover coming up the lane at speed she thought she had inhaled too much smoke and was hallucinating. Then she saw who the driver was and just for a moment her heart pounded a little quicker. Jez jumped down, frowning with worry, as he asked quickly: 'Are you all right? I came over as soon as I saw the smoke. I left my car blocking the road and came up in yours. Luckily you left the keys in.'

'I need to move these animals and we haven't got long,' she said, looking fearfully behind her. 'If the wind gets any stronger we'll have no chance of getting them away. It will be easier with two of us. If we use the Land Rover and the dogs and one of us is on foot we might be able to round them up. I've been trying to get them into small groups but I don't think we've got enough time now. It's all or nothing,' she added grimly.

'You drive, you look all in,' Jez took the crook from her hand. 'I'll run for a bit. The flames have moved around to the far side of the crag so there's really only one way for them to go. Let's try. We'll circle them and when you give the signal we'll all move in.' He opened the back of the Land Rover and the dogs jumped up.

As she drove across to the crag the air filled with the stink of hot rubber as her tyres ran over hot ashes: they were closer to the flames here than they had been before and the dogs whined with anxiety.

'Nearly finished, good dogs,' she soothed. 'Just one more run and then, if we're lucky, that will be all.' Parking the Land Rover she positioned the dogs carefully and then whistled with the last ounce of strength left in her. Off the dogs sprang, they seemed to sense that this was the final attempt and there was an edge of desperation to their ducking and weaving. Jez worked on foot, blocking off an escape route and she drove the Land Rover to slowly complete the circle.

As she watched the flock begin to move, the leader reaching the gate as the last stragglers left the crag, her throat tightened with emotion and relief. They had done it! She followed the flock slowly in the Land Rover, making sure that not a single lamb got left behind.

When she finally reached the lane she found Jez shutting the gate. 'Sheep are surprising animals,' he said with a grin. 'Look at them, they're starting to graze as if nothing had happened. What do you think started the fire?'

Wiping the sweat and soot from her face with the back of her hand, she wearily shook her head. 'I don't know: a discarded bottle magnifying the sun's rays, a cigarette end: with this weather and lots of visitors litter is a real problem.'

'I phoned the fire brigade before I came over, they have a big moorland fire raging on Boulderworth Moor but they said they would come when they could.'

'It will burn itself out soon,' Martha said sadly. 'Then our summer grazing will be gone. Anyway, thank you very much for your help. I couldn't have managed without you. Will you come down to the house for a drink?' she offered shyly. It was a small peace offering but he smiled and nodded.

'Oh, Martha,' her mother said when they got back to the kitchen. 'I've been so worried. I could see the smoke. I phoned the fire department but they said someone had already reported it. What has happened to the sheep? Oh, your poor father. He's spent years building up that flock of Mashams.'

'They're fine, Mam. We got them all off the moor and into the top field. We didn't lose a single one,' she added proudly. 'Ross and Dolly were wonderful. Mum this is Jez, he helped me.'

'Come in, I'll make you a cup of tea,' her mother said with relief. 'How very good of you to help Martha, it's not easy moving a big flock on your own.'

'Mam, I'm going to hose the dogs

down and check their feet, I'll be back in a minute for my tea.' When she got back Jez was sitting at the table eating scones, his blond hair was wet where he had washed and he was laughing: laughter made his eyes crinkle, made him look like a boy and showed his white teeth. Resolutely trying not to look at him, she self-consciously splashed her face and hands under the kitchen tap, listening to the conversation going on between her mother and Jez: they were talking about valley people, the folk who had lived and farming in these parts for generations.

'They don't get together very much any more. The lake divided the valley in more ways than one,' her mother remarked. 'But they all came along to your Dad's send off. It was a real tribute to him.'

Martha, who was pouring out tea, jumped and nearly missed the mug.

'Yes,' Jez said. 'There was a good turnout, he would have been very proud. I'm sorry I didn't have a chance to speak to you that day.'

'I was telling Jeremy about your Dad's arm,' her mother turned to her. 'He says he'll give us a hand with the farm work.'

'I don't need a hand,' Martha said hotly. 'If you look after Luke I can manage fine. I used to help Dad all the time in the holidays. I know what needs to be done.'

Her mother shook her head slowly: 'Lass, your Dad works all day every day and he never gets finished. It will be impossible to do it alone. And valley folk have always helped each other out in times of need.'

'But you're off to Nepal!' Finally she turned and faced Jez, meeting his eyes, defiant and scared at the same time.

'Cancelled,' he said with a lopsided grin. 'And Allan gets sick of me under his feet. Honestly you will be doing me a favour. I might pick up a few clues about farming. Unlike you I never helped at home and my ignorance is legendary. Please let me help, Martha.'

'That's very kind of you, Jeremy, and a weight off my mind,' her mother said, ignoring Martha's agonised expression. 'There's the baby crying,' she added, cocking her head. 'I'll pop up and bring him down.'

They were left alone in the kitchen, facing each other. 'Please don't do this to me . . . ' she said.

'All I'm asking is to help with the farm work. I want to be a good neighbour.'

'My father hates you,' she whispered.

'But your mother doesn't.'

'He'd be angry if he knew you were here. He will detest the thought of you working with me.'

'I don't think so, maybe at first, but he will come round to the idea when he finds out what a help I've been,' Jez laughed aloud. 'That is presuming that I will ever be a help. You might find that I am more of a hindrance.'

Closing her eyes she tried to shut out his smiling face: it was so difficult to remember that she was angry with him when she was faced by his good-humour. 'I suppose I shall have to accept,' she said ungraciously. 'I must go and see Luke before I start the milking,' she turned to leave, avoiding his eyes.

His voice stopped her at the door: 'Martha,' he said gently. 'Drink your tea before you go. Then I'll come and help you with the milking. Will it be very tiresome teaching me?' He was holding out her untouched mug of tea.

'Yes, monumentally so. And I am a very bad-tempered teacher,' she said, grabbing the mug from him and gulping some tea down.

His laughter rang out: 'You liar. You are endlessly patient and kind. It shows on your face.'

Just at that moment her mother appeared with Luke in her arms: 'My, it's good to hear laughter in this old kitchen,' she said with a smile, holding the baby out to Martha. It was then that Martha realized what a gloomy time her mother must have had in the last few weeks, sandwiched between a husband bowed down with work and worry and a daughter who was the same. Taking the baby in her arms she buried her face for a moment in the soft warmth of his shoulder.

'I'm going to help Martha with the milking,' Jez told her mother.

'Then you'll stop and have some supper with us,' her mother added.

'I expect Jez has things to do . . . ' Martha said quickly.

'No, I should love to stay for supper,' he said with a smile. 'I'm getting sick of my own cooking.'

They didn't talk while they organized the milking. Martha was loathe to admit it but he was a help. Inexperienced although he obviously was he had gentle hands and a kind manner which the cows responded to. And after she had instructed him they worked together in a companionable silence. After the milking they fed the calves and the hens and then it was time for Luke's bath. Martha very nearly asked Jez if he wanted to help with that too, but seeing Jez with Luke caused a curious pain in her, a mix of emotions which she could not place but which disturbed her. Seeing him holding the baby in strong male arms and laughing made her very aware of what she and Luke were missing. So she didn't offer and he stayed in the kitchen with her mother where she could hear them laughing and talking.

After supper he asked: 'Will you walk down with me and look at the old village? I think most of the trippers will have gone by now.'

'Yes, I think I'd like to see it.'

'Thanks for today, Martha,' he said as they walked down the hill. 'I've learned a lot already. I had no idea dealing with animals could be so rewarding and such fun.'

'Your family is like mine, they have been farmers for generations. It must be in your genes even though you've tried to reject it.'

'Yes, I always thought the last place on earth I would live would be Reithdale. I have travelled all over the world trying to forget about home. Now I find that when I can finally be free of it, sell up and start afresh somewhere else, I have a curious reluctance to do so. It's as if something calls to me . . . Does that sound silly?' He laughed and looked into her face.

'No,' she smiled. 'Some things you grow into and some things you grow out of. Maybe you've grown into Beckwith Farm and rural living.'

'That's a wise comment. Have you grow in to anything?' he asked curiously.

'No but I've grown out of some things . . . ' she said shortly.

He didn't ask what things, and she wasn't going to tell him, but there was something about him which inspired her to confidences.

'I've grown out of Toby and unequal relationships,' she said firmly. 'I'm getting a divorce and it's not going to be easy. I don't want any complications in my life.'

'Do you see me as a potential complication in your life?' he asked.

When she refused to answer he said: 'We have the potential to be much more than friends, you're not a fool Martha, you can feel it too, can't you?' He stopped and taking hold of her arm gently pulled her around to face him. 'Are you warning me off?' he asked candidly.

An unexpected blush covered her face. 'Yes,' she said. 'Yes I am.' It was only as she finished speaking that she realized her hands were balled into fists and she was completely tense.

'Okay,' he said quietly. 'You won't have to tell me again, Martha. I promise you that. If anyone makes the first move it will have to be you. But I do want to help you. Not just for you, but for your mother and father and for Luke. You must trust me enough for that, please.'

Turning away, she bit her lip to stop the tears. 'I don't have much choice, working today with you made me realise that I do need help and no one else has offered,' she knew the words sounded ungracious but her heart was too full for her to say what she was really feeling.

Jez laughed: 'Okay. So I can stick around as I'm useful. Well that's enough for me.'

As they came through the clump of trees and came face to face with the dried out valley she gasped with amazement. 'Is it as you remember it?' she asked.

He shook his head. 'Now it is finally exposed it is a very sad sight. Somehow even when there was a little water it gave it dignity. Now it is left with nothing it has become just some very muddy ruins. Your father won't have seen it and I'm pleased about that. I think it would break your heart if you had loved this place.'

They walked slowly over the black

dried mud and down to the stream which still trickled along the valley bottom. It was possible to see the curved stones of the old bridge and the foundations of the farm house.

'It makes me feel cheated to see it,' she said slowly. 'Until today I have been unable to walk over the land where my ancestors toiled. Now it's just ruins. It is a lost place,' she shivered, despite the warmth of the evening. 'It makes me sad seeing it. I think my family have been sad since it happened. My Dad told Ruth that the water was going to come in slowly when they filled the valley to give the little animals and birds time to get away, but according to Mum she cried for the whole day when it happened because she said the ants under the stones in the yard would not be able to escape . . . '

Jez looked away across the valley and didn't answer for a moment. His mind was full of his father's letter and of the burden of blame which he felt he carried. He reached out and took Martha's hand. 'I'm sorry . . . ' he said gently.

'You've nothing to be sorry for, it wasn't anything to do with you, you were only a child at the time . . . ' her eyes were bright with tears. 'It's a terrible thing to wish that you could turn the clock back. I mustn't do it. I mustn't wish I had lived at Bridge End Farm and that my family had never moved. It is so futile and negative.'

He nodded sympathetically and said: 'Sometimes we can't help but mourn the past, if you feel you lost something in your life then you need to grieve before you can let it go. I know that well enough. I feel I lost something precious when the valley was flooded.' There was a long pause before he added. 'If it had never happened I might have met you before you married Toby De Leon.'

Moving swiftly she covered his mouth with her fingers, aware as she did so of the closeness of their bodies and of the warmth of his lips on her skin: 'Don't say it,' she whispered. 'It won't help. Some things can't be undone and all the wishes in the world won't change them.'

Without speaking again they turned and walked up the hill together in silence, a careful distance between them.

# 4

Sunlight streaming through the open farmhouse door dappled the quarry tiles of the floor with a dancing yellow gleam and the kitchen was fragrant with the smell of newly baked bread and scones. But, despite the tranquillity of the setting, Martha was sitting at the scrubbed table frowning with worry and chewing the end of her pen with an anxious air as she checked rows of sums. Jez, walking passed the window, saw this little scenario. Obviously the account books made depressing reading because he saw Martha shake her head and close the book with a sigh. When they were seated at the kitchen table with their coffee he asked gently: 'You seem very low, is everything all right?'

Martha looked into his blue eyes and smiled, but there was sadness in her voice as she said: 'Just when you think things are getting better something else pops up — another bill, another repair, another loss that can't be balanced.'

There was a long silence: they had been working together at the farm for weeks now and a companionable relationship had grown up between them so that they could talk or be quiet together. He waited, sensing that she wanted to talk.

'Susanna seems to have sorted Toby out.' Martha confided. 'He has finally paid the mortgage and signed a contract on the house. The sale should go through pretty quickly, so I seem to be winning on that front. But the farm finances are in a real mess. I don't know if we can last until the house sale goes through. Even then I expect I'll have problems with Dad because he won't want me to plough the money back into the farm. But things are so bad the bank has threatened to withdraw our overdraft facility. I don't know what I'll do if that happens. I don't think I'm making a very good job of running the farm,' she added gloomily.

'You're doing a marvellous job,' Jez encouraged. 'It's the weather which is to blame. There's no grass, so we're having to use winter feed and buy it at hyped up prices because of the demand. Then there are all the fly-borne diseases which need the vet and antibiotics. Allan's having exactly the same problems as we are.'

'Is it the drought that is making life so expensive?' she asked wistfully.

'Yes,'

'But how do people manage? How does your farm manage?' Martha asked, an edge of desperation in her voice.

Jez looked away, his face serious. He didn't like to be reminded of their differing circumstances. Martha had even offered to pay him for his help at the farm which had caused him some anguish. He would have liked to have reached for his cheque book and written out the amount which would cover the broken tractor, the feed bill and the vet's account but he knew that was impossible.

'We diversify,' he said. 'There are several redundant farm cottages converted into holiday homes. And we have a caravan site and farm shop at Cragdale Woods. Most farmers need to find another use for their buildings or land these days.'

'Well we haven't got anything we could use . . . just a burned-out moor and a car park, Martha said sadly.

Jez's eyes lit up with sudden enthusiasm. 'You've never shown me your work. Do you have any paintings of the valley? Or of the farm or the dogs?'

'Yes, but why?' she asked.

Jez reached across and gripped her hand. She didn't resist this touch and just for a moment he savoured the feeling of her small hand under his. He smiled at her as he said: 'Because the one thing we have got at the moment is endless visitors and lots of them would buy a picture to remind them of their visit to the lost valley. Let's have a look at your paintings.'

Martha was suddenly shy as she pulled out the folders from underneath her bed. 'Honestly Jez, my work is mediocre in the extreme. Toby always used to say I painted birthday card scenes.'

'How very elitist of him,' Jez said grinning. 'Did it never occur to him that most people like birthday cards, that's why they buy them?' Looking down at the selection of oil and water colours she had laid out on the bed he beamed: 'Martha you are sitting on a gold-mine. These are absolutely perfect. Look, there's even one of the reservoir . . . and the colours are magnificent.'

'But Jez there are so few of them which are worth selling, some of them aren't even finished. And even if I managed to sell them I haven't any more and I certainly don't have time to paint at the moment or even to make copies.'

'Oh,' Jez laughed. 'I'm not suggesting

we sell these. They would be far too expensive for most day trippers to buy. No, I've got a friend who makes fine art prints. We would have fifty prints made of each picture and then sell them ready framed.'

'Don't tell me. You have a friend who does framing as well?' Martha said suspiciously.

'Yes, and it will be very inexpensive because of the numbers. Leave that to me.'

'But what happens if we don't sell them?'

'We'll sell them, trust me.' He leaned across and drew out a water colour she had painted of her mother's herb garden where lupins and pansies grew among the chives and parsley. 'I love this one, Martha. It is breathtakingly simple but so charming. People will love it.'

They looked at the picture together: just for a moment their arms and shoulders touched, but then she moved away shaking her head in disbelief. 'I didn't even bother to show that picture to my tutor. Every one else at college was experimenting with bold new ideas. It was considered so old fashioned to paint flowers and people — Toby used to tease me like mad.'

Not for the first time Jez felt a wave of anger against Toby De Leon rise up in him and he bit back a bitter retort. He felt that slowly Martha was beginning to trust him and he didn't want to destroy that. She was, he knew, fiercely loyal, and she never complained openly of Toby's treatment of her. But Jez guessed from the few times she had spoken that Toby had drained her self-confidence. He looked down at the paintings, even the most gentle of the water-colours had sudden bursts of brilliant colour: a blood-red poppy among a vase of flowers, a vivid sunset over a sombre sea. He felt they echoed Martha's own nature; gentle and self-effacing, but with a streak of steel resolve and a fiery temper.

'I think your paintings are wonderful,'

he said gently. 'You have a very real talent.' And, holding his breath in case she moved away, he reached across and caressed her bent head. 'I wouldn't say it if I didn't mean it.'

She looked up, startled by his touch, and met his eyes: 'I know that,' she whispered. 'Thanks, Jez. It means a lot to me that you like them.'

Stifling the urge to sweep her into his arms and kiss her soundly, he said practically: 'Well, let's make a selection and I'll take them into Skipton. We need a table and a sun-screen, then we can set up a stall in the car-park.'

'But no-one has time to sit up there selling pictures,' she protested as Jez began sorting the paintings into piles.

'One of Allan's boys has just finished his GCSEs and is kicking his heels. He's asthmatic so farm work is too heavy for him. It is a holiday job which will suit him down to the ground.'

'I can't believe this is happening,' she said.

Jez laughed. 'You'll believe it when

it pays the vet's bill and puts four new tyres on the Land Rover.'

★ ★ ★

Two Sundays later Jez received an invitation to Heather's home. The request for him to be there to meet up with his sisters was made in a voice which brooked no refusal.

He was the last member of the family to arrive, because he insisted on helping Martha with the morning chores before he set off. After he had parked his car in the farm yard among the Range Rovers and Jeeps which his sisters drove, he was swamped by the younger of his nieces and nephews who rushed out to kiss and hug him.

'Out into the garden please,' Heather said firmly to the children who were swinging on Jez's arms and chattering. And, as if on cue, the various husbands herded their offsprings into the garden so that he was left alone in the kitchen with his sisters. Accepting a glass of lemonade he looked at their serious faces saying with a grin: 'Is this the interrogation room or are you the firing squad?'

'We're worried about you,' said Rosemary gently.

'We're not cross with you. We haven't asked you to come here for a telling off,' Heather added. 'You're too old for that anyway . . . '

'I'm glad you've realised,' Jez quipped, looking sideways at Lydia. He knew his sisters well enough to know that she would be the one to make the first move.

The was a silence while Lydia sipped at a glass of dry sherry gracefully then said: 'To be honest Jez, it was the photograph in the local paper of you and the Hetherington girl and the article about the sale of her paintings that has worried us.'

Jez, deliberately misunderstanding her, interrupted her with a grin: 'Oh don't worry about that project, Lyd. It is all going splendidly. We are on a second print run for some of the pictures. The visitors love them. We've sold hundreds.'

The sisters exchanged looks and Lydia added 'We'd heard you were going over to help out at the farm.'

'Which frankly,' Heather added, 'we found astonishing.'

'Why? It's something I want to do,' Jez said quietly.

'In the photograph . . . ' Lydia said, returning to the original topic like a dog to a bone, 'you had your arm around her and you both looked well . . . you know what I mean.'

'Do I?' Jez said, drinking his lemonade down and putting the glass on the table. 'Look, my lovely sisters. This is the story. I am helping the Hetheringtons out with the farm work while Mr Hetherington recuperates and I helped Martha organize the sale of some of her pictures to boost their income. The local press coverage was a real boon and I was pleased to be in the picture. I am very fond of Martha.'

He paused and smiled rather sadly. 'But she is married and trying to get divorced, she's been through a hell of a time and her baby is still very young. The last thing in the world she wants is another relationship and she doesn't want to know about me . . .'

'Well, you both looked very much in love in the photograph.' Lydia snapped.

'Maybe we did,' Jez said with a small smile. 'And they do say that the camera never lies.'

Heather sighed. 'We know her father is away at the moment. We just want to warn you. There will be hell to pay if he finds out you have been seeing his daughter. You're too young to remember but there were lots of very angry scenes about the flooding of the valley.' Heather looked embarrassed and then added: 'I shouldn't really say this, it's speaking ill of the dead, but Dad betrayed him.'

'Oh let's not rake all that up again,' Rosemary, the quietest and most gentle of them said. 'It's all in the past. Please.'

'I think he needs to know,' Lydia said, dangerously quietly. 'It might make him see sense.'

Heather sighed: 'Jez you were probably too young to realise what a mess Mother and Dad's marriage was in. I can only assume that he was driven by a desperate desire to get rich and buy her the kind of life she so desperately wanted.' There was a pause and Jez realized that none of his sisters would meet his eyes. Heather continued slowly:

'Dad got to know about the plans to build the reservoir some time before anyone else. Instead of letting the other farmers in the valley know he started buying up land. We were always better off than the Hetheringtons and it was easy enough for him to buy up some of their really poor quality woodland with the story that he was going to drain it and replant it. The Hetheringtons have always sailed close to the wind financially and they were offered a good price. The old man didn't want to sell but Dad and he were good friends and I think there was some talk of a joint venture when the new wood was established. Deeds changed hands . . . Then, of course, when the plan for the reservoir came out there was a great deal of anger.'

'Dad did nothing illegal. It was all above board. Hetherington ruined himself with legal bills . . . ' Lydia protested. 'When Dad heard about the plans it was just a rumour and it would have been irresponsible for him to spread it around. And he'd always had a policy of buying up any scraps of land which came on the market.'

Rosemary intervened: 'Lydia. We mustn't rewrite history. Dad knew that the land he bought was vital because it gave access to the valley. And he also knew that once he decided to sell and back the plan there was no hope for the other farmers. The reservoir made Dad very rich. Unfortunately it wasn't enough to keep Mother . . . '

Jez put his head in his hands, deep in thought. 'So the Cragdale Wood access road, the caravan park and the shop, all of them highly lucrative, would have belonged to the Hetheringtons if Dad hadn't duped him?' There was a moment of silence in the room. All his sisters were avoiding his eyes. Finally he said: 'Dad left me this.' He took the letter from his pocket. 'He asked me to make amends to the Hetheringtons. I didn't really know what he wanted me to do, or why.' He passed the letter to his sisters and they read it in turn.

'What you must realise, Jez,' Lydia said softly. 'Is that there really can't be any friendship between our families. There is too much double dealing and hurt from the past. Old man Hetherington will never forgive you for being a Davies. I just hope to goodness you're not getting involved with Martha Hetherington. Don't try to be friends with them, please. It would be much better to leave well alone.

You'll only make things worse.'

Jez rose to his feet. 'I think I'll give lunch a miss, if you don't mind, Heather. I want to go home and think about this.'

'The children will be so disappointed . . . ' Lydia said.

But Rosemary smiled gently and said: 'You go if you want to Jez, you've obviously been working hard. You've lost weight.'

Before he left Jez turned to the three women and said quietly: 'Thank you for telling me the truth at last. It might have been better if Dad had told me himself or at least put it all in the letter. But at least now I know what I'm dealing with. I feel I owe the Hetheringtons a debt of honour and helping out with the work for a few weeks is a mere drop in the ocean. I warn you I'm going to try to put things right and you may not like the way I do it.'

There was embarrassed laughter from them: 'Is that a threat?' Lydia asked. Jez smiled and shook his head: 'Just letting you know . . . '

Even though he wasn't due at the Hetheringtons until the evening milking he drove straight there. Part of him wanted to pour the whole story out to Martha and beg her forgiveness: but part of him wanted to spare her from the revelations that her father had been duped and deceived because she'd obviously never been told the whole truth behind the family feud.

What he craved more than anything was her nearness: the sight of her face and the soft timbre of her voice. Gradually over the weeks Martha had trusted him enough to let him look after Luke, to be present at bath and bed time. And this growing relationship with the child coupled with seeing his nephews and nieces had made him realise that he wanted more from life than to always be on the outside looking in — borrowing a little corner of someone else's life. He made a decision that he would level with Martha and tell her the whole story — there had been too much deception in the past. He longed suddenly for everything to be straightforward and easy between them. Then, when she was ready, there might be room in her life for him . . .

As soon as he arrived in the farmyard he knew something was wrong. Martha's car was parked by the back door and it was piled high with cases and bags. Knocking on the back door, he tried to think of some rational explanation as to why she appeared to be leaving home. As she answered the door he said with an attempt at cheerfulness: 'Are you going on holiday . . . ?' but his words trailed off as he looked into her face. She was pale and drawn and her eyes were puffed up and red as if she had cried herself sick. 'What on earth is the matter? It's not Luke, is it?' he asked suddenly terrified.

Shaking her head she turned away from him, as if the sight and sound of him hurt her. He pulled her into his arms, folding her against his chest, feeling the sobs running through her body. 'Tell me,' he whispered burying his face in the softness of her hair.

'It's Toby. He phoned and told me he is going to apply for shared custody of Luke . . . ' She clung to him then, as desperate as a drowning woman. 'I just couldn't believe it. He said he would be coming next weekend and would take Luke back to London. But he doesn't lead the kind of life which fits in with a baby . . . I couldn't let him look after Luke. Toby isn't like other people . . . he loses all sense of time when he's painting and often works through the night, drinking wine. He's so careless about everything except art. He might give Luke the wrong kind of food and choke him. And then, when Luke's crawling . . . there are so many hazards. Toby would just laugh if you talked about stair-guards or not leaving dangerous things about. I'll have to go back . . . It's the only way.'

'Go back . . . ' Jez said uncomprehendingly. 'You're going to go and talk to him about it. But why can't you do that by phone, or get Suzanna on to it?'

'I phoned Suzanna. She said it was almost definite that Toby would get access and visiting rights. He is Luke's father . . . Not that you would think so,' she added bitterly. 'He's never bathed him, or changed a nappy. He hardly looked at him when we were in London. But now . . . now when he realises that the house is going to be sold he suddenly wants him back. I'll have to go back to him, Jez.'

'You don't mean you're going back to live with Toby?' Jez felt as if a hand of ice had grabbed at his heart. 'Why? Tell me why, Martha?'

She raised her tear-stained face to his and her hands came up and clung to his neck. 'I can't trust Toby to look after my baby . . . '

'He won't always be a baby,' Jez whispered.

'Can you imagine what life will be like for him if I don't go back and he has to split his life between me and Toby. Every other weekend away with his father, weeks of the summer holidays away from home. How could he have a normal life or friends if he is constantly being ferried between us? Toby knows I won't agree to it.'

'There must be a way around it. Surely you don't have to go back to him,' Jez said desperately.

'Toby doesn't love Luke, or me. He has thought this up because he wants me back — I was too useful. I paid the bills. I cleaned the house. I was a good housekeeper. That is what he wants back. I may as well give in. He is quite unscrupulous enough to use Luke as a pawn and I won't allow that. If it means living a sham of a marriage with someone I detest in order to give Luke a settled home I'll do it. I can't hand my baby over . . . I just can't . . . '

'Let me come with you, you're in no state to drive,' he pleaded.

'There's the milking and the calves . . . '

'I'll phone Allan, his boys are home for the holidays. Ian is an agricultural student, he'll come and take over. I must come with you.' To his relief Martha didn't argue, she seemed in a daze of misery. Her mother came down with the baby and they strapped him into the back of the car. 'Sit in the front with me,' he begged.

The Sunday afternoon shimmered in the heat and all around them were the sights and sounds of a country summers day: high in the sky the larks were singing and a pair of curlews flew over in the fields, mewing out their strange haunting lament. The roads were busy with cars, families out for picnics, their children in bright T shirts holding faces to open windows for coolness. It all seemed so ordinary and natural.

In a moment of futile anger he wondered why their life should be so out of time with everything else. Why weren't they a happy couple who would go home with their baby to a little house somewhere, unpack their cold box and then, in the cool of the evening, sit on the lawn and drink cool beer and talk about their day?

'What are you going to do when we get to London?' she asked, suddenly fearful.

'Don't worry. I'm not going to cram Toby's elegant teeth down his throat. Much as he deserves it!' Jez said grimly. 'I'll go to see my agent — she's been asking me to visit her. She's a good enough friend for me to just drop in on. Then I'll get the train home. I'll help your mother until your father is back to full health. If necessary I'll dye my hair and wear a false beard so he doesn't know I'm a Davies.'

'Oh Jez . . . ' she said with a little laugh that soon turned into a sob. They sat cocooned together and, when they stopped to break their journey, he carried the baby into the motorway services cafe. She walked next to him with the distracted air of an accident victim.

'I'm sorry,' she said, looking down at the sandwiches and salad he placed before her. 'I don't think I can eat anything.'

'Just drink the coffee then,' he said sympathetically. When they had finished feeding the baby they both knew it was time to travel on but neither of them moved, as if reluctant to carry on with the final leg of this journey. 'What will your marriage be like do you think?' he asked at last, a frown shadowing his eyes. 'You can tell me to mind my own business if you want, but I would like to know.'

'I want you to know,' she looked directly at him, her green eyes dark as a stormy sea with unshed tears. 'It will be totally empty. A marriage in name only. Toby and I were finished, bar the shouting, as soon as he reacted so badly when I got pregnant. I didn't need to find the receipts to know there was someone else. He never came near to me after I said I was going ahead with the pregnancy. He's slept in the spare room since then. Is that what you wanted to know?' She held his gaze and he dropped his eyes first, looking down, biting his lip:

'I'm sorry. I don't know why it matters so much but it does. I don't want him to have all of you. It seems so unfair.'

'I wish there was some way out, but I have to do this for Luke. Maybe later, when he's older I will be able to get away. I'll go back to teaching, get a flat nearby. Then I can live a separate life . . . '

Taking hold of her hand he held it gently for a moment: 'I hope so, Martha. I really hope so.'

He parked the car at the top of the road where she lived. 'I'll get out here and walk back to the tube,' he said, and taking a notebook from his pocket, he scribbled down a number. 'This is where I'll be for the rest of the day. My agent lives in Richmond.

I'm not far away if you need me, so just phone if there's a problem. I'll be travelling home at about six o'clock I should think.'

'I don't think there'll be a problem . . . ' she said uncertainly. 'I'll try to ring you tonight at home just to say . . . ' her voice faltered. 'To say goodnight or something.'

Just for a moment her control snapped and she threw her arms around his neck. 'Thank you for coming with me, Jez. It's so hard to say goodbye.'

'Don't say it then,' he whispered, smoothing the hair back from her face and beginning to kiss her forehead, her eyelids and her cheeks with tiny featherlike brushes of his mouth. 'Say you'll come to see me when you're next at home, promise me that?'

'Yes, yes, I will . . . ' she breathed, and then they kissed like lovers — lips searching mouths, fingers tangling in hair, as they pressed ever closer to each other.

Finally they pulled apart, breathless, their eyes wide and almost frightened, as if they both knew those kisses had fuelled the spark which had smouldered between them for so long. 'Hell and damnation, Martha, this is madness, utter madness,' he groaned.

Then the baby woke and began to cry and Martha turned to the back of the car, hiding her face and the tears streaming down her face: 'Please go, Jez, this isn't making it any easier for me.' And he got out of the car and walked away without a backward glance.

At the top of the road he stopped and turned back to look at the street of narrow cramped houses and small front gardens. Martha's house stood out because of the big window in the attic which was Toby's studio. The London street was dusty and littered with drink cans and McDonald's boxes. The plane trees and overblown roses in the gardens were wilting in the summer heat, and the combined smell of traffic fumes, food and too many people in too small a space made the air heavy and stale. It was so horribly different to the farm with its high moorland fields, fresh air and birdsong. He couldn't bear to think of her being imprisoned there, walking everyday with Luke passing rows of parked cars and shabby suburban gardens, rather than down the farm lane where cow parsley waved like a lace cover over the drystone walls and lapwings circled the fields.

With a muttered curse he retraced his steps, walked up to the front door of Martha's house and leaned on the bell. It was a long time before anyone answered. When Martha finally came to the door she looked at him blankly for a moment as if she didn't know who he was. She looked wild, like a creature who was cornered, tense and vibrating with some extreme emotion. Pulling the door closed she grabbed his arm so hard it hurt: 'Thank goodness you are here. I was going to ring you,' she whispered fearfully.

'What ever's the matter?' he asked. Her hand on his bare arm was hot and trembling now.

'Everything!' she whispered, glancing behind her to check that the door was still shut. 'I've got to get home . . . '

'Get home?' he questioned. 'But you've only just arrived.'

'I've made the most terrible mistake.' Her green eyes were dark with misery. 'Toby has a woman here and he doesn't want me back. He wants Luke. You have to help me, Jez. They want to take my baby away from me.'

Before he could answer he heard Luke start to wail. She turned and ran back into the house and he followed quickly. The ground floor was an open plan kitchen and living area. The back door was open to let in cool air and he could see a small garden and a high brick wall at the back of the house. The furniture inside was functional and rather shabby, very ordinary, apart from the walls which were crowded with modern paintings, testimony to

Toby's talent and prolific output.

Toby, who was barefoot and dressed in jeans and a striped T shirt, was sitting sprawled on a settee, laughing. Luke, who was screaming, was being held by a plump middle-aged woman wearing a sleeveless sun dress and too much make-up.

'Oh darling . . . ' she was saying in an affected way. 'What is it that you want? Does Daddy know?'

Toby laughed again and shook his dark hair from his eyes. 'Oh, come on Sarah, your guess is as good as mine.'

'He's hot and hungry and his nappy needs changing,' Martha said angrily, taking the baby from the woman's hands. 'I'm going upstairs . . . '

'Take Sarah with you,' Toby called, reaching for a bottle of wine on the table. 'She needs some lessons in nappy changing . . . By the way,' he turned to Jez with narrowing eyes. 'Who the hell are you? Have you just wandered in off the street or do you want a drink?

I know you, don't I?'

'We have met,' Jez said icily. 'Jez Davies.'

'Oh, the photographer chappie.' Toby grinned. 'There are some glasses over there, help yourself. Why are you here?'

'I drove down with Martha. We are neighbours in Yorkshire.'

'Oh, old friends!' Toby mocked.

'Good friends,' Jez said, with an underlying menace in his voice.

Martha and Sarah clattered back down the stairs. Sarah was talking non-stop about decorating a room and how splendid it was. 'I need to heat up Luke's bottle,' Martha said in a tight voice. Jez held out his hands for the baby but Sarah got in first.

'Come to me, sweetheart,' she crooned. 'Come to Auntie Sari.' Jez saw a spasm of pain pass over Martha's set face and she took the child with her into the kitchen. Sarah was still talking, rattling away like a runaway train, and Jez wondered when she stopped for breath: 'Well,' she was saying. 'The colour is robin egg blue but that is the only aspect which is traditional. But then we like to be a little bit different, don't we, Toby?' Turning to Jez she asked: 'Would you like to come upstairs and see the room we have decorated for baby.'

Jez followed Sarah's plump back up the narrow stairs. 'So, you've helped Toby with this, have you?' he asked genially. 'It's beautiful, obviously it's had a woman's touch.' He actually thought the geometric shapes and patterns were hideous but he wanted information from Sarah. 'Are you an artist?' he asked, walking across to the window and looking down at the rows of narrow back gardens. The room was stuffy and smelt of paint. He wanted to throw open the window and breathe some clean air. Even with the window closed he could hear the noise of traffic and children shouting.

'No, I used to dabble a little when I was a girl and I have a very good eye for what is fashionable. I run the Mykonos Gallery. You may have heard of it.' Jez nodded and she looked pleased. 'I love Toby's work, we have been friends for years. And now, well, since he's been on his own, we've just clicked. It's been marvellous.'

Jez turned and looked hard at her. Her makeup was running a little in the heat and the smudged kohl around her eyes and her over-lipsticked mouth gave her a clown's face. She was certainly a great deal older than Toby. 'My husband died six months ago and I didn't think there would ever be anyone else. But Toby and I have both been bereaved in a way. He was absolutely devastated when Martha left him. You know at first he gave up any hope of having his son with him. But I said, nonsense, lots of fathers get custody these days. I've always wanted kiddies . . . ' She smiled fondly as she added. 'He's such a beautiful little boy . . . just like his Daddy. Children need their father, don't they?' Jez turned away, unable to find a reply, fighting his anger.

'Despite Toby's talent he has a struggle financially, doesn't he?' he asked at last in what he hoped was a friendly tone.

'Oh yes,' Sarah agreed. 'And it's such a shame. He really is a genius. Do you know, I say to my friends that in years to come I will be proud to have helped him,' she joined Jez at the window and he could smell the alcohol on her breath mingling with her expensive perfume. He turned away from her, pity overtaking his anger now because he realised that Toby had found himself a meal-ticket and Luke was to be the payment.

Sarah had obviously decided he was a confidant, because she shyly held out her left hand. There was large emerald and diamond ring on her third finger. 'He's such an impetuous boy. He sold a painting in New York and blew the lot on this for me, wasn't that sweet?'

'Yes,' Jez said, with a forced smile.

'Just as well he's got you to pay the mortgage.' Sarah laughed as they made their way downstairs.

'Of course, we'll have to have a nanny, I couldn't possibly give up work. But the darling child will have a better life here in London. I mean, there really is nothing to do in the country, is there? Nothing which stretches the intellect. We've sold this house and my flat is on the market so we'll find somewhere bigger with a garden in a good area.' And, just for a second, Jez felt a moment of utter rage at the way Martha's contribution to the house had been forgotten.

Downstairs Martha was walking in distracted circles with Luke who was screaming with the high pitched cry of a baby in pain: 'He's got colic . . . ' she said despairingly to Jez. 'He's in agony, he keeps pulling his little knees up and arching his back. I've given him some gripe water but it hasn't helped. Will you hold him while I run a warm bath? We'll put him in that and let him kick his legs about, it might help.'

'Oh poor little darling,' Sarah said, pouring herself a glass of wine. 'What an awful din.'

'Is he going to keep that noise up all afternoon?' Toby asked fretfully, pouting like a child. 'I was hoping to work . . . '

'Sweetheart!' Sarah cooed. 'You can't work on the first day that baby is here. I thought we'd take him for a walkies in the park . . . '

'I hate the park on Sundays — it's too crowded,' Toby grumbled. 'If I can't work I'm going to the pub, at least it is cool and quiet there.' He rose to his feet and patted his pocket to check he had money. Finding he didn't, he turned to Sarah with a scowl. 'I'm out of change. I can't even afford a beer.'

'Oh . . . ' Sarah cried, her face soft and crumpled with distress as she reached for her handbag. 'Here, darling, take this . . . ' She handed over a twenty pound note and Toby

140

reached across and took it while at the same time kissing her cheek.

'When I've got Luke bathed and fed I'm going,' Martha said quietly.

'Going? Where are you going?' Sarah said, looking puzzled.

'Home. To Yorkshire!' Martha snapped.

'Oh, have we got everything here we need for baby?' Sarah asked with a frown of worry, reaching into her bag for a packet of cigarettes. Then, thinking better of it, she put them back.

'I'm not leaving my baby here with you,' Martha snarled at her, her eyes glinting with rage. 'Not now — not ever. You can fight me in the courts if you want to, Toby. But I shall tell the world you aren't fit to be a father. You didn't want Luke and you made my life hell when I refused to have an abortion.' Sarah's mouth fell open with astonishment and Toby tried to speak but Martha overrode him, her voice was low but relentless. 'You started an affair when I was pregnant. I tried to make myself believe that it wasn't so and I stayed, hoping you might see sense, hoping that being with your son might make you grow up. But it didn't and when I found out you were still seeing that girl, and spending money on her while bullying me about working full-time, I made up my mind it was the end. And you shan't have Luke. You're not spoiling anything else in my life . . .'

'This isn't true? Is it, Toby? Who is this girl?' Sarah asked, her voice quivering with shock.

'Of course it isn't true.' Toby snapped. 'She is totally neurotic. It's all in her mind. I'm not staying here to listen to her insane ravings. I'm going out. I'll be back sometime!' He strode out of the house and, after giving Martha an agonised look, Sarah gathered up her handbag and raced after him.

'Let's get Luke bathed and think about what we can do?' Jez suggested. Then, when the baby was in the warm water and had quietened down, he asked: 'Who was the girl Toby had an affair with?'

'Oh,' Martha said wearily. 'It was a student from the Art college where Toby teaches. He brought her back a couple of times, saying he was using her as a model. I knew he was trying to upset me and tried to ignore it.'

'But he doesn't paint pictures of people, life studies or portraits.' Jez said with narrowing eyes, thinking of the geometric shapes of Toby's pictures.

'That's why I thought he might be involved with her . . . but then the visits stopped and I didn't want to make a fuss. We were living separate lives and I just wanted to get through my pregnancy without another crisis.'

'Can we get into his studio?'

'Well, I know where he keeps the key,' she said doubtfully, wrapping the baby in a towel and putting him over her shoulder. 'But he hates anyone going in there and he goes berserk if even a pencil is moved. I never even cleaned it . . . except for about once a year when he would watch me like a hawk in case I spoiled anything.'

'Oh dear,' Jez said with a grin. 'Well poor little Toby is in for a bit of a shock because I want to have a snoop around. How long do you think he will be at the pub?'

'Hours . . . ' Martha said. 'Hold Luke. I'll find the key.'

Once upstairs Jez began to systematically search the cupboards and drawers. There were hundreds of drawings and paintings and, as he leafed through them, he hoped his hunch was right. He racked through piles of canvases, and folders of sketches, but there was nothing but Toby's usual strange abstracts. At last he had searched everywhere, including the desk drawers, but there was nothing at all incriminating. Nothing which proved Toby had been unfaithful to his wife.

Jez looked around the room, frowning, wiping his forehead with the back of his hand.

'Why were you so sure we'll find something?' Martha asked.

'Because if an artist falls in love with a woman then he makes something in her image . . . ' Jez replied, thinking of the photograph of Martha in an antique silver frame on his bedside table.

'Maybe he didn't fall in love . . . ' Martha said quietly.

Jez looked around the room thoughtfully. All the pictures he had pulled out were now in untidy heaps. 'Hold the baby. I'll have to try to tidy up.' Martha said.

'Wait a minute . . . Do you have the keys to that filing cabinet?'

'It's full of receipts and bills not pictures,' she said reaching into the desk drawer for the key.

'I'll try anyway.'

The sketches were hidden away at the back of a filing cabinet. 'They're not very good,' Martha said critically. 'I'm surprised he didn't throw them away.'

'He obviously didn't have his mind on his work,' Jez said with a shrug. 'But it's lucky for us he didn't. How many are there? Twelve? Enough to make a lovely little display for Sarah.' He looked down at the pictures and laughed: 'Toby signed them so nicely and put her name, Melissa, and the date on them, how very helpful.'

'Oh Jez . . . ' Martha said, following him down stairs. 'Do you really think any of this will help?'

Jez nodded: 'The pictures aren't very good but they show a rather lovely young girl and Sarah knows enough about art to realise the significance of a well known abstract artist suddenly taking up life studies in charcoal like a second year art student. I think she is the one who wants Luke here so they can play house together. Finding out that Toby is capable of lies and double dealing will at least warn her and might make her see your point of view. And as soon as I've put them out, we're going home together. If

146

we set off now we'll be back by midnight.'

'Oh Jez,' she said longingly. 'It sounds so marvellous to hear those words . . . going home together.'

# 5

The sky was darkening as they left London and the air was cooling. It was a relief to get on the motorway and away from the tangle of evening traffic. The baby slept in the back of the car and Martha curled on the front seat looking out of the side window, lost in some private world of grief. 'You forget how terrible the heat is in the city — it's like a furnace,' he said to break the silence between them. To him she seemed fragile, as if the episode with Toby had drained her strength. He found himself wondering, not for the first time, what perverse attraction had drawn Martha and Toby together in the first place. They seemed so ill-suited: the erratic, temperamental artistic genius and the shy country girl who enjoyed painting flowers and dogs.

'Yes, but when you live there you

don't notice it. I suppose people can get used to anything if they have to,' she replied rather sadly.

'It wouldn't have worked out if you had gone back there, you know,' he said levelly. 'You have too much spirit to live a lie. But I do admire you for attempting it.' He didn't know what else to say to try to ease the pain for her. Part of him, selfishly, wanted to know how much she had loved, still loved Toby, and whether deep down she had wanted to give her marriage another try. When he glanced across, he saw that she was fighting back tears and he changed the subject quickly, talking quietly of safe neutral topics.

They stopped briefly somewhere in the Midlands to change and feed the baby and drank bitter grey coffee in the desolate cafe of the motorway services, so it was past midnight by the time they reached Reithdale. 'It's so late. Would you like to come to Beckwith Farm? The spare room is always ready and there is a cot in there. We can put

Luke straight to bed.' He was frowning, trying to think what would be best for her and the baby, because if he was honest, the idea of taking her to his home filled him with sharp pleasure.

'Yes . . . Thank you . . . Mam needs her sleep. I think it would be unfair to wake her at this hour.'

The house was in darkness when they pulled up outside. 'Wait here,' he said softly as he got out of the car. Then he was back, crossing the gleaming river cast by the outside light, to help her from the car and carry the sleeping child. She stumbled with weariness as she made her way into the immaculate kitchen. 'I'll get Luke settled and go straight to bed,' she said wearily.

'You must eat something. You've had nothing all day.' Jez remonstrated. 'There are clean towels and a robe in the bathroom next to your room. I'll show you where everything is. Have a soak and unwind.'

'Yes, you're right. I think I would

feel better for a wash and some food,' she said with a grateful smile. He took her upstairs and then returned to the kitchen. He worked with swift economical movements and soon had a meal organized. When she returned to the kitchen he had laid out cutlery and blue china and was busy at the Aga frying an omelette.

Peering into the pan she smiled, saying: 'That smells good. I didn't realise I was so ravenous.'

'I've opened a bottle of wine and there's hot bread over there on the table. Have a nibble until this is ready,' he said, smiling down at her: dressed in his oversized navy bath robe with her damp, freshly washed hair coiling over her shoulders she looked like a little girl.

She padded over to the table and sat down. As she began spreading thick yellow butter on the baguette she said thoughtfully: 'This morning I thought my life was over and now I'm here back here in Yorkshire. Going down to London seems like a bad dream.'

Jez deftly dished up the omelette and served her with tomato salad. 'You'll feel even better after some food and a night's sleep.'

'Half a night's sleep,' she joked, looking up at the clock. 'It will soon be time to start the milking. But it's so good to be back. Up until now I hadn't really decided where I would live. To be honest I hadn't thought any further than keeping the farm going until Dad came back. But having taken Luke back to London I know I don't want to live there, with or without Toby. I want to stay here, in Reithdale, and I want this to be Luke's home too.'

'That's a good start,' Jez said in a neutral tone. 'It gives you a fixed point and I think you must insist that Toby fits in with what you feel is best for Luke, so access visits would be here until Luke is old enough to have a say in what he wants to do.'

'Have you ever been married?' she asked suddenly, he laughed and replied:

'No. I would have told you about it if I had.'

'You've never told me much about your personal life. Have you ever been close to marrying someone?' she persisted. He was aware of her watching him closely as he took a mouthful of food.

Smiling across at her, he said gently: 'Afraid not. Watching your parents tearing each other apart when you're a kid rather dents your confidence in relationships and I've spent most of my time travelling. Running away, I suppose.'

There was silence while she ate her omelette, then she said slowly. 'Isn't it strange that for all these years we've lived so close to each other. Our houses on opposite sides of the valley. Yet we never met. And then we landed back here at the same time. Like birds blown in shore by a storm.' There was a pause and then she added, 'And nothing has ever been clear or easy between us, has it?'

'No,' he said thoughtfully. 'It's been a case of squalls and gales when we get together.' Pretending to be absorbed in his food he didn't add that their feelings for each other also had elements of the fierceness and heat which had dominated the natural world since they first met, but she had never accepted it. 'There's the problem of Toby and the antagonism between our families. Sometime, but not tonight, we have to talk about that.' Jez said quietly. He was tempted to say more, but, looking across at her, he saw that her eyelids were drooping with weariness. 'Come on, off to bed,' he chided gently. 'I'm going to clear up the kitchen.'

'Aren't you tired?' she whispered.

'No. I'm a bit of a night owl. I often work through until dawn.'

'There's so much I don't know about you,' she said wonderingly. Then, to his amazement, she leaned across and kissed his mouth. It was nothing more than a fleeting touch of her lips. 'Goodnight, and thanks for everything,' she muttered, as if she regretted her impetuousness, and then she disappeared quickly upstairs to bed.

* * *

The sunrise woke her in the morning. She had been so tired the night before she hadn't pulled the curtains. For a brief second she couldn't remember where she was. Above her was a pale primrose ceiling and not the sloping white of her room at home. Then she remembered — she was at Beckwith Farm with Jez — and she sat up looking around the room curiously.

The rooms of the farmhouse were large with big square windows. This room was decorated in blue and yellow with cheerful floral curtains. The old wood floor had been polished to a dark hue over the years and was covered with a selection of fine Persian rugs. The furniture was a mixture of dark woods. Nothing really matched and yet the whole effect was very pleasing. Obviously most of the pieces had been in the family for years and had simply landed up in the guest bedroom.

Slipping out of bed she looked out of the window. Already the farm was working — she could hear voices and the purr of machinery — but what really held her attention was the fact that the room overlooked the valley so she looked upon a familiar scene which she had never seen from this vantage point. Leaning out of the window she wondered if it was possible to see her own home, but it was tucked behind the curve of the hillside and all she could see was the copse and the top moor.

Breathing in the cool morning air, she noted the heat haze lacing the valley in a smoky veil, and knew it was going to be another hot day. Then she heard Luke wake up, yawning and giving a little mewing cry. Lifting him high she kissed his face, luxuriating in his warm milky scent. A surge of relief that Toby had not taken him from her filled her eyes with sudden tears of thankfulness.

Later, after bathing and changing Luke, she was drawn to the kitchen by the fragrance of fresh coffee. Looking across at Jez she wondered how much sleep he'd had because the kitchen was clean with the table set for breakfast and Luke's bottle was waiting on the Aga. Jez was freshly showered, his hair still wet and gleaming gold, and he was standing by the kitchen door looking through his post.

'Come on in, the coffee is on,' he said with a smile. 'Would you like toast or bacon? Here, let me hold him,' he said, holding out strong capable hands. 'And you test his bottle.'

They were sitting at the table and Jez was feeding Luke a lightly boiled egg when the phone rang. It made her jump because she hadn't noticed the small white telephone on the work-top. Jez's face hardened as he took the call. 'It's for you,' he said rather grimly, handing the phone over to her.

'Sorry to disturb you and lover boy,' a voice drawled. 'Are you breakfasting or still in bed?'

'Oh Toby,' she said wearily. 'Don't be childish. And how did you know I was here?'

'Oh, it was very simple. I put two and two together.'

'And made five,' she snapped.

'It didn't take you long to find someone else, did it?' Toby said with thinly disguised malice. 'You've been gone only two minutes and now you're shacked up with Jez Davies. So much for your holier-than-thou attitude. Or was all this going on before you left? How long has he been an old friend exactly? Tell me, is the kid really mine?'

'What on earth are you talking about?' she retorted angrily, stung by his words. 'How dare you accuse me of living by your alley cat standards. And, as for getting shacked up with anyone, living with you for five years has put me off the idea of having another relationship — ever!'

Toby laughed. 'Oh dear, quite on our moral high horse, aren't we? I just thought you might like to know I've been offered the share of a studio in New York and have decided to take it. London has become rather drab and my creative juices seem to be drying up. I need a change of scene.'

'Oh it will be a great relief to get rid of you!' she retorted heatedly. 'Good riddance.'

'Just don't start asking me for money for the brat,' Toby said with sudden open hostility. 'I'm not getting lumbered with paying for it. You better leave me alone or I shall contest paternity in court and cite Jez Davies as the father.'

Before she could answer he hung up and she was left holding the receiver, her mouth a round 'O' of astonishment. A rush of emotion swept over her. As in the moment of death her life seemed to replay before her in seconds. Her first meetings with Toby, his pursuit of her, her feelings of reverence and love for his enormous talent and obvious need of her. The years of looking after him, nurturing and caring for him as if he was a child and she a mother. And now . . . now this utter rejection of his own son, their combined flesh and blood. She realized that before this morning she had been angry with Toby, hurt by him, and out of love with him. But this was death: a complete cessation of any kind of feeling. No room for anger or pity just a terrible blankness.

Dropping the phone as if it were hot, she jumped up from the table and paced across to the open door. 'God in heaven, what have I done to deserve this?' she questioned blindly, trying to control her turbulent feelings. All she could find within her was grief. Toby had outflanked and outmanoeuvred her. Not only had he denied being Luke's father but, by doing so, he had contaminated her relationship with Jez.

Then, looking up, she saw Jez's set face, and the shuttered look in his eyes made her realise that he had been imprisoned in the kitchen, the baby on his knee, unable to escape from the one-sided telephone conversation which had hurt him.

Dumbly she held out her hands for the child. Jez handed him over and then walked past her out of the door and across the farmyard. She opened her mouth to call him back, but no sound came. And so she stood miserably in the sunlight, watching his denim-clad figure disappear from view. Even if she called him back she didn't know what she could say to make things right between them.

They travelled in silence as they drove to Moor Top Farm. The radio and Luke crowing filed the emptiness. She was just gathering her courage to speak as they drew up into the yard. 'I need to talk to you, Jez. Somewhere quiet . . . ' she said slowly.

'Yes, I need to talk to you too,' he

said and then added. 'But it seems you have visitors.'

'It's Ruth's car,' she cried with surprise. 'Dad is back!'

Jez was holding out the baby to her. 'I think I'll go and check on the lad I left in charge. Allan dropped him over here first thing this morning and he's had all the chores to do.'

'They've seen us now,' she was waving to a row of faces in the window. 'You must come in. They'll think there is something wrong if you don't — that we have something to hide.'

'There are things I wanted to talk to you about before I saw your father,' he said reluctantly. 'But you're right, come on, in we go.'

★ ★ ★

For a while in the kitchen there were only hugs, cries of delight and exclamations on how much Luke had grown. Then a sudden silence. Martha took hold of Jez's hand and pulled him forward to the centre of the kitchen. 'Dad, Ruth. I want you to meet someone who's been helping me run the farm. I couldn't have managed without him. Dad — this is Jeremy Davies.'

'I know who it is, lassie,' her father said quietly. 'And I've vowed in my time that no Davies would ever set foot over the doorstep of this house again.' His tone wasn't rude or aggressive but she recognised that icy tone from her childhood. Ruth and the boys had suffered it more than she had: that cold severity which brooked no argument, which was deaf and blind to all pleading.

'Dad,' she interceded desperately. 'Jez has been a friend in a million. He worked every day to help me. And yesterday, when I had to dash to London to see Toby, he arranged for Ian to cover for us and drove me down and back. Please try to understand . . . '

'I spoke to your husband this

163

morning, Martha, and I understand plenty. You're a married woman and it's not my place to tell you what to do.' Her father paused ominously, his mouth curling as if something bitter had tainted his tongue. 'All I'll say is that if you want to spend nights over at Beckwith Farm there's no place for you here with us.'

There were startled gasps from her mother and Ruth and Martha's face flamed. 'It's not what you think at all, Dad. It's just Toby trying to make trouble,' she said miserably. 'And I don't see why I should have to explain myself in front of everyone like this — it's humiliating and unnecessary.'

Jez took hold of her arm in a quick gesture of support and said quietly: 'There are two issues being discussed here. One is any relationship between Martha and I and the other is who I am. As far as the first goes I am very fond of Martha. So fond, in fact, that I wouldn't dream of taking advantage of her. She was very upset yesterday and

I was worried about her driving all the way to London with the baby. When we arrived back last night it was too late to do anything but stay over at my home. And I give you my word that I would do nothing to insult her or our friendship.'

Her father laughed, a grim dry kind of sound, as he said softly: 'I've had the word of a Davies given to me before and I'll tell you what it was worth — it was worth nowt! So don't give me your fancy promises.'

Jez's face hardened and his tone was terse as he continued: 'That brings me to the second point — who I am. Presumably if I was any other friend of Martha's, who had helped her out and given her a bed for the night, there wouldn't be a problem. I would give you my word that I wouldn't take advantage of her and you would pat me on the back and say: 'Of course you wouldn't, lad, you're one of us.' But you don't say that — you are prepared to accuse me of lying simply because of who my father was.'

'Aye, happen I am.' Her father said truculently. 'Now there's the door, and take that young whippersnapper of a lad with you. If I'd known earlier where he'd come from he wouldn't have milked my cows.'

'Oh Dad,' Martha said, her voice rising with a sob. 'How can you behave like this? It's so unfair . . . '

Jez put his arm around her and said softly: 'It's not unfair Martha. He has every right to treat me like this.'

Martha turned into his shoulder for a moment of comfort, dashing tears from her eyes with her fingers. 'It's all so pathetic, still quarrelling over the stupid reservoir . . . as if it matters now,' she added bitterly.

'It isn't just that. There's much more.' Jez said slowly. 'I didn't know the full story myself until yesterday. Up until then all I knew was what Dad told me in a letter he left with his Will, which made it clear Dad was only too well aware of his wrong doing and wanted to make recompense. But he was so ashamed he didn't tell me much. My sisters filled me in on the full extent of his treachery.' Jez took his wallet from his pocket and pulled out the letter, and handed it to the other man. 'I'd like you to read it, Mr Hetherington, because when he was dying his thoughts were for you. I think it was his way of asking for forgiveness. Although he wanted me to be the one to obtain it.'

As the letter passed between their hands Martha said in a puzzled voice: 'Is there more that I don't know about?'

'Aye, just a bit,' her father said bitterly. 'I was robbed and made to look a fool. I handed over deeds for very little money. Then when I tried to fight it out in court I lost. Any compensation money got eaten up by the lawyers — they got richer than any from the whole sorry mess.'

'And your father asked you to make up for all this?' She turned to Jez her eyes flashing with some unfathomable emotion.

'Yes,'

'So that is why you have helped me with the farm work?'

'Partly.'

'I see.'

Her father was reading the letter. He shook his head slowly when he reached the end of it. His wife said gently: 'It was such a long time ago, Sam, the lad was still in short trousers. You can't hold it against him. Jez has been a real friend to us. We'd never have coped without him. He's saved the farm for you, that must count as something.' With a sigh she added. 'It's your pride which is still hurting. But there was never any shame in trusting a friend. And it happened all those years ago . . .'

'Aye, well, you're right, as always.' Her father said, sucking in his cheeks and thinking deeply. Finally he turned to Jez and asked quietly: 'I'll thank you for the help you've given me and my family. And I'll hold out my hand to you — this once.' And there was silence in the kitchen as the two men shook hands. Jez wondered if Martha realized the implied threat in the words 'this once'. Obviously he had won a battle but not the war . . .

★ ★ ★

The heat that day was terrible. The sun burned with such ferocity that the world seemed burdened by the sultry air and animals and men appeared to move in slow motion. There was no breath of a breeze — not even on the top of the moor. And the sides of the valley dried like a desert with cracks running like crazy paving across the black mud.

Martha went down to the bottom of the valley in the cool of the late evening, drawn by habit and a desperate need to get out of the house and Ruth's endless questioning. She knew her sister only meant to be kind, but she was too raw and hurting to want to talk. She had also felt strangely redundant. Dad was back in charge and she was not needed anymore. Dad had taken over the jobs she had got used to doing, and back in the house she found that Mam and Ruth were only too eager to look after Luke so she was helped endlessly. All this on a day when she had wanted time alone to think.

The sky was a wonderful deep midnight blue and the moon was a shiny silver sixpence. The air was still thick and hot but she breathed in the scent of grass and animals gratefully, walking swiftly, glad to be alone and outside.

Some primitive instinct told her that Jez was waiting in their usual meeting place when she reached the bottom of the valley. Sensing rather than seeing him, she was aware of his presence even before the dogs realized he was there. For a moment she was tempted to turn and leave before he saw or heard her: and she stood for a moment, torn between desperately divided emotions. But then Dolly and Ross got his scent and began barking a welcome. Hearing his voice out calling her name she knew it was too late and that she could not walk away from him.

'I think it's going to rain at last . . . ' he said in greeting.

'Yes, there's thunder in the air. It will be a relief if it does,' she answered stiffly, thinking to herself how ridiculous it was talking about the weather when her heart was thudding with pent up emotion.

'I'm packing up. I'm going abroad on an assignment,' he said with equal reserve, patting the dogs and not looking up at her.

'I thought, I mean, you'd said you were going to try living at Beckwith Farm . . . ' If her heart had been thudding before it was now racing as if she had been running and her voice was no more than an uncertain whisper.

'Oh, I'm just in the way there . . . It's

been fine while I've been over here all the time but Allen doesn't want me breathing down his neck. He's been used to doing things his own way. I've got interested in the farm but I can't just take a back seat and be a gentleman farmer. It's not in my nature. So I've taken a job in South America. The fellow who's been doing it has fallen sick and they need a replacement straightaway. It will be hard travelling. I think it's what I need . . . '

His words had an eerie echo of her morning conversation with Toby and she closed her eyes to try to blot out the pain of rejection she felt. 'Yes well, you've done everything you wanted to here, haven't you? Tried out farming — found it interesting. Patched up your father's old quarrel and redeemed the family pride. Quite an achievement.' Her tone was sarcastic and he turned sharply to look at her, but she swung her head away, letting her hair fall in front of her face.

'In fact you are quite wrong. I

feel I have achieved very little,' he said quietly. 'I am interested in the farm, but I'm not sure that is enough. And I haven't managed to heal the breech with your father. So it's very unsatisfactory.'

'I thought you'd been happy here . . .' she said moodily, moving away from him as she spoke.

'Nothing has made me unhappy, but you've made it obvious from the start that you don't want a relationship. I'm nearly thirty, Martha, I don't want to be hanging around you forever like some love-sick boy.' He was laughing at himself, making a joke out of it all. His endless good-humour suddenly made her angry. She was hurting and selfishly she wanted him to be hurting too.

'It fitted in so neatly, didn't it?' she said bitterly. 'There I was, a damsel in distress, who just happened to be the daughter of your father's old enemy. And there you were, on a mission to make up for past ills. It makes me sick to think of it frankly.'

'Why does it make you sick?' he asked, suddenly serious. Taking hold of her arm he gently pulled her around to face him.

'Because you've patronised me and used our friendship. It wasn't for me — it wasn't anything to do with me. You helped me because of who I am. Because I'm Martha Hetherington!' she shouted angrily. 'I thought it was for me! I thought you did it for me!'

Above the deep cleft of the valley came an ominous rumble of thunder. The dogs watched the sky as the moon and stars were swallowed up by inky-black clouds. Lifting their faces they were rewarded by the first slow heavy drops of rain landing on their faces and open mouths. Martha was too engrossed in her anger to notice the fast-approaching storm. It was Jez who said: 'It's starting to rain.'

'Oh! I don't care,' she flared back at him.

'What do you care about?' he asked,

refusing to take his hand from her arm. 'It isn't Toby, is it?'

'No it isn't,' she retorted furiously. 'To be honest marriage to him was like being a household slave and it's only now I'm free that I realise how utterly miserable I was.'

'You'll have to be very careful that experience doesn't spoil the rest of your life. You don't trust anyone now, do you Martha? And you should try it sometimes.' There was a thread of strong emotion in his voice which fuelled the tension between them.

'You aren't in a position to give me advice!' she said, stung by his tone. 'And as you are off on your travels, running away again, we can call this goodbye. Well, thank you very much for all the help you've given me, but don't try to tell me how to run my life.'

Pulling away from him she would have walked away but, taking hold of her hand, he turned her back to face him. 'This is goodbye,' he said firmly.

And he swept her into his arms and kissed her mouth.

The storm was overhead. With a loud crack the clouds burst and rain came down with a sharp rattle like machine-gun fire. Above their heads thunder clapped like an explosion. The dogs jumped to their feet and began to whine but Martha was oblivious to anything but him. Returning his kisses, she found her anger transforming into a far deeper emotion. Her hands moved up and tangled through the damp gold of his hair as she explored the hard muscles of his neck and caressed the evening stubble on his cheeks. His fingers returned her caresses, stroking her face and smoothing the rain back so it soaked down onto her hair.

Caring nothing for the deluge streaming in cold rivulets down her face and hands she clung to him as if she would never let go. And, as the storm raged, they stood oblivious to anything but each other, kissing and stroking, their soaked bodies pressed so close they were wrapped together in a glistening skin of rain.

The dogs, agitated by the roaring boom of the thunder and the lashing rain, were barking at the sky. Maybe it was this noise, or the flash of lightning which lit up the heavens and filled the valley with an unearthly light, which finally brought Jez to his senses and made him pull back from her. She was still dazed, lost in some world where only the touch of his lips and skin existed, as he cupped her face with his hands. His mouth hovering inches from her lips. 'Just say one word, just one, and I'll stay,' he implored her.

Dumbly she shook her head. He kissed her mouth lingeringly. 'Please . . . ' he begged. Again she shook her head.

'Okay. I didn't really think you would . . . ' He turned and, taking her hand, began to pull her up the hill. Suddenly, she was aware of her soaking clothes and the crashing storm. She was shivering from the chill of the rain, shivering because all the warmth and closeness of his body had been taken away and replaced by harsh reality.

At the farm gate he finally let go of her hand: 'God bless, Martha,' he said in parting, and then he was off, lost in the swirling darkness of the night, jogging through the rain in the direction of Beckwith Farm.

For a moment she watched him go with disbelief, unable to comprehend that she really had refused to ask him to stay. Thoughts, fears and anxieties crashed through her mind. She had nothing to offer in a relationship — she was penniless, jobless, homeless and there was no chance of a welcome for him at her parent's home. If he stayed they would start a relationship. She licked her mouth which felt hot and swollen from the passion of his kisses and knew that a love affair between them was inevitable. But what about Toby and Luke . . . the problem of paternity suits and recriminations? That would be a wonderful scandal for Reithdale to chew over. She could imagine the reaction of Jez's sisters and family to it all. It was all such an impossibly bad start for anything . . . It was wisest to keep to her resolve and let him go. She needed to get her life into some kind of order.

But her heart was not wise. Suddenly she ached for him with every fibre of her being so that her body and face where he had touched her felt unbearably naked and alone. Every nerve in her body wanted him so much that she was breathless. And in that moment of wild longing all her fears and reservations vanished. She knew she wanted him, needed him and that they must not be apart. He had asked for one word and she gave it to him now. She called his name, shouting into the wind: 'Jez . . . Jez . . . come back, please.'

But the night was full of wild sounds: the creaking of branches flaying in the wind; the lashing of torrential rain on old slate roofs and rock-hard earth; and finally the monstrous roaring of the thunder shaking the ground with each crash. All these conspired to whip her desperate words away and smother them in the darkness.

Following him down the hill she started to run, her sandalled feet slipping in the mud, calling for him until she was breathless. When she reached the copse of trees she knew it was useless. Her hair was so sodden she could hardly see when it fell across her face and her sandals were water-logged. Jez, in training shoes and with a head start, would be home by now. Biting her lip to stop her tears of disappointment, she called to the bemused dogs who were watching her with sorrowful eyes, and made her way home.

Her parents were in bed. Quickly, she changed out of her soaking clothes, towelled her hair dry, tied it back and checked on Luke. She would have liked to have set off then but her conscience made her dry the dogs and mop the pool of water she had left on the kitchen floor. After that, she pulled on her raincoat, which was stiff from lack of use, and set off again down the hill. It was easier walking in wellingtons and she soon reached the bottom of the valley. Within minutes she had rounded the curve of the hillside and could see the lamps of Beckwith Farm shining across the valley. They seemed to be guiding her to Jez; and, despite the slippery terrain, her footsteps quickened and she was soon breathless.

The rain had slackened slightly and the thunder had moved across to the other side of the dale. As she walked she heard it rumbling and crashing in the distance as the eastern sky was rent by a bolt of lightening.

Stopping to draw breath she realized that it was becoming increasingly difficult to walk. Her boots were clogged with mud and she wished she'd had the forethought to bring a torch so that she could pick a drier path across the valley. She had been spoilt by clear moonlit nights and had forgotten how dark it could be when low clouds descended. But the flickering lights of Beckwith Farm were nearer. She felt that she could almost reach out and touch them . . . all she had to do was follow the welcoming glow and she would get to Jez.

So determined was she to follow a straight line that not even the heavy walking made her stop. But when water almost filled her wellington boots she halted abruptly and looked around her. Her eyes had become accustomed to the darkness. The clouds were lifting and she could see enough to realise, with a gasp of horror, that the deluge had filled the stream. It was no longer a trickle meandering along the bottom of the valley. The torrential cloudburst had returned it to a fast-moving stretch of water. She could hear a rushing torrent of water — and she was standing in the edge of it. Another step and she might have lost her footing completely.

Common sense, and her instinct for survival, made her move slowly back onto firmer ground. Finding a stone, she sat down and slid her feet from her waterlogged boots. If the rain continued the valley would soon become a lake again — an impenetrable obstacle to Jez. If she wanted to see him that night she would have to go home, get the car out and drive the twelve miles around the top of the valley. The most sensible thing to do would be to phone, but she didn't know if she could say the words which were racing through her mind on the phone. She felt she needed to hold him and tell him that she loved him.

Her eyes longingly watched the lights at the other side of the water. Then, slowly, one by one, they went off. Until, finally, the far side of the valley was in utter darkness. Then she saw smaller lights moving, slowly at first, then more quickly. She knew immediately they were the headlights of a car but she did not want to accept what she had seen.

Buoying herself up for the long upward climb in the mud she told herself that it must have been Allan, or one of his sons, leaving the farm. She did not want to believe that Jez had left. It was only when she tried to telephone him and the phone rang and rang in the emptiness of Beckwith Farm that she admitted the truth. They had been divided once again by the water — the valley which had brought them together had finally parted them. Jez had gone. He had turned his back on Beckwith Farm, and on her, and she had no one to blame but herself.

The tears she cried were bitter and fell as hard as the rain which lashed the valley. Now the rain had arrived the lake would reappear. And she and Jez would be divided, as they always had been in the past, by that long deep stretch of blue water which symbolised all the past events which had conspired to keep them apart.

★ ★ ★

Autumn arrived with the rain and summer was over. Within days the leaves began to fall and the wind which whistled down the length of Reithdale had a chill in it. The cold dourness of the shortening days fitted her mood. The sudden drop in temperature made her long for activity and hard work — to keep warm and to keep the demons at bay.

It was not only in her dreams that Jez haunted her. But at night she had no control over her unconscious and in the long weeks after he left she often awoke in the morning with tears upon her cheeks. As the weeks lengthened into months the dreams did not fade or lose their power to hurt. But she found that with an effort of willpower she could use her misery to fuel her daytime energies. She wanted to be independent and she wanted to make a future for herself and Luke. So she became determined that in one area of her life she would have success, and found that a broken heart does not stop you from working hard . . . quite the reverse. Her work became her solace and refuge. But Jez was never far from her thoughts and in the early morning and the long watches of the night she would remember him, and think about the long hot summer when, like ghosts, they inhabited the forgotten valley; walking, sitting and loving in places that were now drowned and gone, covered by a sheet of grey water, lost under white-capped waves and dark curtains of rain. And it seemed to her that, like the valley, the love between them was also lost and forgotten.

# 6

When Jez touched down at Leeds Bradford Airport the cold hit him like a physical blow — it was like being in a boxing ring. Blasts of icy air seemed to levy punches at his face and neck and made his chest ache. He knew that the sensible thing to do would be to go home, have a hot bath, and find some winter clothes instead of shivering in his lightweight tropical suit and raincoat. But his mood wasn't sensible. And so it was easy to by-pass his home and tell the taxi driver to carry on into town because no one even knew he was arriving. He'd grabbed the first seat on standby and, in the rush to leave, hadn't bothered to telephone his family.

So now, as effortlessly as a ghost, he slipped into town in the early darkness of the January afternoon. He was like a man possessed, so driven that even the cold ceased to bother him. After the heat of the tropics he rather gloried in it and the challenge it presented to his body. Also he didn't want to be comfortable. His mind was too disturbed and it somehow suited his dark mood to be chilled through to the bone.

For the first time in all his years of travelling coming back to England gave him culture shock. He realized that he had been so taken up with his thoughts during the long flight back that he hadn't registered the passing of time or negotiated the usual sign posts which told him he was returning. The journey was a blur but now suddenly he was acutely conscious of his surroundings.

He noticed the bright lights of the shops and the garish red SALE signs which adorned most windows as he wandered through the streets of the town, hunching his shoulders against the cold. He had only the briefest of descriptions of the shop he wanted but he was determined to find it. Several times he asked people, but most were strangers or locals who didn't know its whereabouts. So he trudged on, desperately aware of the lateness of the hour. If he didn't find the shop soon it would be closing time and then he would have to wait until the morning. Having travelled so far he was filled with surging impatience. He found he was jogging along the footpaths, diving down side roads, and peering into courtyards. It was good to run, it warmed him a little and it made him feel as if he was in charge.

At last, in a narrow ginnel running down from the main shopping street, he found THE ART WAREHOUSE. With a small smile he realised the joke in the name as it was the smallest shop in the town, a tiny narrow building squeezed by some early builder between two larger buildings, with an elegant miniature bow window and doorway so low he had to bend his head to get in.

Once inside he looked around with amazement. It was incredible that so much material could be stored in such a small place. The shop was indeed a warehouse, the simple shelves were stacked with boxes and there were wire baskets for shoppers to choose their purchases from the shelves and bring them to the cash till. With a rush of disappointment he realised that the dark-haired girl sitting behind the till was not Martha. He had thought, hoped, he would find her here. Breathlessly he leaned against the door frame, trying to subdue his impatience and disappointment.

'I'm closing in a minute,' the girl said with a smile. 'But you've got time to buy, providing you know what you want.'

'I haven't come to buy anything,' he admitted.

'We've got the new timetable for the art classes,' the girl said automatically, reaching for a leaflet at the side of the till and handing it to him. 'There are some additional ones starting but they are very over subscribed.' She smiled kindly at him as he looked down without comprehension at the piece of paper in his hand. 'Sorry, I thought you wanted classes,' she said, reading his thoughts.

'I want Martha,' he blurted out, more truthfully that he realised. 'Is she here?'

'Yes, I'll call her.' The girl locked the till, moved passed him to the door, flipped the open sign to closed and made her way to a narrow stairway. 'Martha,' she called. 'There's someone to see you.' Then turning to him she added. 'You can go up, she's in the workshop. Tell her I'll lock up.'

The stairs were narrow but the room at the top was surprisingly spacious. The ancient floor had been stripped and varnished and the lighting was so finely tuned that it was like walking into a place full of sunshine. Martha was standing in the middle of the room, surrounded by a semi-circle of empty easels. Her abundant hair had been tied back and coiled at the back of her head and she was dressed in an ancient paint-smeared smock and jeans.

For a moment they just stared at each other, the air empty with silence. She seemed too shocked to smile and her eyes were guarded: 'Hello Jez, this is a surprise. I'm just getting everything ready for my next class,' she said finally, with an attempt at normality.

'When is your next class?' he asked urgently. 'I need to talk to you.' He had horrible visions of a troop of people arriving just when he had found her. He felt he might explode from impatience if that happened.

'Not until tomorrow,' she whispered, avoiding his eyes and wiping the paint-brush she was holding on a piece of damp rag. His sudden appearance had obviously upset her and he could see that her fingers were trembling as she made the pretence of finishing off the task.

It was the sight of her small white
fingers fluttering with agitation which
sent his emotions into overdrive. With a
muttered exclamation he moved across
the room and took the paint-brush and
rag from her fingers. 'Why are you so
frightened?' he demanded.

'It's just such a surprise to see you.
And you look so . . . I don't know.
You can't just turn up out of the blue
and not expect people to be startled by
the sight of you . . . '

'Could it be a bad conscience that's
making you afraid?' he asked grimly.
She turned her face away, in the
brilliant light of the room, he could
see that the long sweep of her lashes
were suddenly pearled with tears.

'It's just a shock,' she whispered.
'You are the last person in the world
I expected to see. In your Christmas
card you said nothing about coming
back. I thought you were away until
the summer.'

Oh,' he said with a shrug. 'At
Christmas I didn't know what I know

now. Are you going to explain it all to me, please Martha?'

Turning back to him she lifted her face defiantly to his, her mouth a stubborn line as she replied sharply: 'What exactly would you like explained, Jez?'

His face was hard-edged and his voice taut with emotion as he said: 'Lydia wrote to me. It takes time for gossip to reach her but when it does she is very prompt in passing it on. She wrote and told me that people everywhere are saying that I am Luke's father. It appears to be a statement of fact not just speculation. And I seem to be the last person on earth who has been told of this!'

Her eyebrows raised as she retorted: 'Well, you have been away in the jungle. Are you surprised that news travels slowly to the Amazon basin?'

Jez sighed with exasperation: 'Don't be flip with me, Martha, please! This is important to me.'

She looked straight at him, her green

eyes held his gaze. 'I have constantly denied to the world that you are Luke's father, unfortunately it has only made the rumours fly faster.' A look of genuine despair flashed across her face and it hurt his heart to see it. Her voice dropped to a husky whisper: 'I can only apologise to you, Jez, and say how sorry I am. But there really was no need for you to come half way across the world to pick a fight with me about it. And you shouldn't have come to see me. It will only make people talk more. Hopefully in time the gossips will find someone else to torment and leave us alone.'

'Heavens above, Martha,' he interrupted irritably. 'Surely you don't think I've come to find you because I was worried about what people are saying?'

'They're blackening your name, first in London and now here. Saying that you got me pregnant, ruined my marriage and then left me. It is horribly degrading for both of us, but Toby was determined to have his revenge.' Bowing her head, she wiped her eyes with her fingers, angrily dashing away the tears which had risen to her eyes. 'I am more than sorry about it all, Jez. If I could turn the clock back and erase it all I would. Especially as you have been so good to my family — and to Luke.'

'Hell and damnation,' Jez said, his temper erupting suddenly. He walked over to the window as if driven by demons. It hurt him to be standing so close to Martha and not take her in his arms. 'All that was meant to be strictly confidential . . . No one but your father, the solicitor and I were meant to know about it.'

'Oh Jez,' smiling through her tears she added: 'How little you know of small towns. You go away to South America and then the next thing we hear you have signed the deeds of Cragdale Wood over to Luke and made his grandfather responsible for the income from the shop and caravan park. You can't do something exceptional like that and keep it secret. Of course it got out. It was the talk of the town and everyone was agog. They all had ideas on how Dad should spend the money. It was as if he'd won the Lottery! Now we all know why you arranged it so that Dad had the benefit of the income until Luke is grown up, but sadly it only fuelled the speculation that you are Luke's father and were paying me off.'

'I hope your father doesn't see it like that,' Jez said stormily.

'No, Dad is one of the few people in the world who understood why you gave the land to Luke. It was land which Dad was cheated out of and it was right it should come back to him. He couldn't have accepted the return of the deeds himself, but by giving it to his grandson you by-passed Dad's pride very nicely and he is grateful for that. The money has made a big difference to him and to all of us. What you wanted to achieve has happened. But your name has been dragged through the mud in the process. Your kindness in wanting to right a wrong from the past has been misunderstood in the eyes of the world. And those of us who know the truth are all very sorry about it . . . ' She was trembling all over now and her eyes were bright with tears.

'Oh, for heaven's sake, don't be sorry about it! I've had about all I can stand of thanks and apologies,' he raged at her with sudden temper. 'Why didn't you write to me when the rumours first started? And why didn't you tell me when Toby first threatened you? It was the morning when you stayed at Beckwith Farm with me, wasn't it? If you had told me then it could all have been so different.'

Standing stiffly she drew her shoulders back and took a deep breath as if suppressing her emotions. 'Yes, I'm sorry . . . I thought it was an empty threat from Toby. I thought he would go away to America and leave us alone. I didn't care that he was refusing to pay maintenance for Luke. I was proud. I thought I could manage alone. I didn't realise he was going to wage a vendetta against you. And how could I tell you, Jez? Try to see things from my point of view. I knew you were an honourable man. I didn't want you feeling any sense of obligation to me. That is no basis for friendship or anything else. I hoped you might never hear of it. I am so very sorry it has roller-coasted into this enormous scandal.'

'For goodness sake,' Jez snapped. 'Will you stop apologising to me! I am not here because I care tuppence for my reputation or what people are saying about me. I am here because . . . '

He stopped in mid sentence. Then he moved slowly across to her. 'I'm here because . . . ' he tried again. 'Because when Lydia wrote and told me what had been happening I was angry with Toby, and angry with you for not telling me. And I was full of hurt and grief that Luke's father didn't want to own him, and you didn't want me.' He lowered his head, suddenly afraid to meet her

199

eyes. 'I love you and Luke.' There was a beat of silence between them and then he continued. 'I love you both so much I used to hope that one day I might be his father. To have people accusing me of running out on him broke me up. I had to come back . . . I had to have it out with you . . . ' As he finished speaking she was in his arms, her head resting against his chest, her hands reaching out to him.

For a moment there was nothing in the world but closeness. At the feel of her small body in his arms a shuddering sigh ran down the length of his body. He held her so tightly it was as if he would never let her go as he buried his face first in her tumbling hair and then in the soft warm hollow of her neck. Then he searched for her mouth, his hands cupping her face so that he could kiss her lips. Finally, breathlessly, they moved apart and she whispered: 'Oh Jez, I wanted to write and tell you, but I was so afraid. I can't tell you how many times I started letters to you, but

I didn't want you to come back to me out of pity.'

'Why didn't you tell me before I went away? If you had I would never have left you to face it all alone. It must have been so terrible — it was as if Toby and I had both abandoned you.'

'I was in such a muddle,' She confessed pressing her face against his shoulder. 'I tried to run after you that last night we were together. But the water had filled the river and I couldn't get across. Then I saw you leave and, when the headlights disappeared, it was like an omen. I felt I had to sort things out for myself. I honestly thought it was an empty threat from Toby and so I just concentrated on getting the house-money from him and starting my business. I thought that was all I had to do. And that then, when you came back, I would be a person in my own right rather than just a charity case. But then, when the gossip started, I didn't know what to do. I had dreamed of you coming home and us meeting up again and starting with a fresh page. Meeting up with no complications in our lives . . . What a hope! The rumours grew and grew. In the end I just had to hope and pray they wouldn't reach you and I could explain it all when we next met.'

With a muttered exclamation of exasperation he pulled her closer and covered her mouth with one passionate kiss after another until she was wrapped inside his raincoat and they both smelt of paint and turps. Finally, when she was pliant and exhausted in his arms, he whispered: 'There's only one thing for it Martha, you'll have to marry me.'

'Oh,' she replied teasingly, pulling back from him and refusing to let him kiss her mouth. 'And why is that? You're not going tell me you've ruined my reputation and need to make an honest woman of me, are you?'

'Well, there's that, of course.' He stroked his fingers down the line of her face, unable to take his eyes from her. 'And Luke needs a good father.'

'Well,' she said mock-seriously. 'I think you'd be a good Dad.'

'But the most important reason,' he kissed her mouth fiercely, his fingers tangling in her hair so that she could not tease him and move away, 'is that I am madly in love with you and I can't live without you.'

'Oh, really?' she smiled. 'Well you seem to be managing all right in South America. Lydia came into the shop and told me you were having a wonderful time and dating a Argentinean heiress.'

'I tried to forget you,' his voice was low. 'Don't think I didn't. I was raw and bitter from your rejection and I really felt angry with you for a time. I didn't see why you couldn't let me into your life. Gradually, I heard what you were doing. You see, Lydia kept me up to date. I know when the shop opened and everything about it. I began to see that you were putting your life together. And, although I didn't want to admit it, I started to see that you wouldn't have been able to do that with me around. You needed space and I had to give it to you. But I can't say that it didn't hurt. I've been so lonely and the more I surrounded myself by people and beautiful women the more lonely I became.'

'I'm very glad to hear it,' she whispered lightly, but her eyes were full of deep emotion. 'If you'd been having a good time you might not have come back to me . . .'

'Oh,' he laughed, taking the comb from her hair and letting the heavy curls fall down onto her shoulders. 'I knew I'd come back to you. It was just that Lydia's letter jet-propelled me with temper and worry.' He pulled her nearer, his hands coiling into her hair so that she was captured and held close. 'But now I want us to be together all the time. I want us living at Beckwith Farm as a family. I want to share your life and you to share mine. Marry me, Martha and let's make it soon.' He kissed her hungrily. She returned his kisses with the same intensity until the room, the afternoon, the very earth was blotted out by their need for each other. Eventually, breathlessly, she nodded her head:

'I'll marry you, Jez. I love you too,' she whispered. 'And right from now, from tonight, we will be together all the time. I've been lonely, so lonely without you. And we've missed too much time to waste a single minute.'

'Do you think your father will give us his blessing? It would mean a lot to me and to my memory of my father.'

'Well,' she kissed his mouth softly. 'Why don't you come home with me and see?'

'At least tell me what you think,' he argued.

'I'm not going to say another word. Mam is expecting me home at six so let's get off. You can stop and have supper with us, then you can see for yourself.'

Jez said, kissing her again: 'Well, your Dad wrote and told me to call when I came home so at least I'll be allowed into the house.'

On the journey he questioned her closely about what had been happening while he was away. Eventually they talked about Toby.

'He should have given you more than half of the sale money — it was your earnings which paid for the house,' Jez said shaking his head. 'It hardly seems fair.'

'When was life ever fair?' Martha said with a grin. 'I didn't begrudge him the money. He's doing well in the States. I'm just grateful that he doesn't want to disrupt Luke's life. And the money was enough for me to get a lease on the shop and stock it. There's a tiny flat at the top of the building, Luke and I sometimes stay there when I'm working. The shop is breaking even at the moment but I'm doing well with the painting lessons and of course the students buy their materials from me as well.'

'Do you have time to paint?' he asked.

'No . . . ' she smiled. 'But when Luke is older maybe I will.'

When they pulled up in the yard outside Moor Top farm he noticed there was a new outside light shedding a welcoming glow across the farm yard. The outside of the house was freshly painted.

'What do you think?' she asked.

'It's looking good.'

'Come into the barn quickly, there's more.'

Proudly she showed him a nearly new Land Rover parked in the immaculate barn. 'It's a good second hand one. Dad is like a kid with a new toy. And we've a better tractor. But what has really made a difference has been buying in new stock. Dad has a vision of a pedigree herd by the time Luke's at school.'

'I knew the money would be well spent,' he said with a smile, slipping his arm around her. 'You don't have to prove it to me.'

'Oh Jez, I can't wait for you to see Dad and Mam. I never knew how worn out they both were with the continual grind of trying to run the farm on too little money. But that income from the shop and the caravan park has given them a new lease of life. Dad is taking Ian on full-time when he finishes at college. He works in the holidays and a weekends at the moment. And the difference it has made is nothing short of a miracle. Come in and see for yourself.'

Any reservations Jez had about the warmth of his welcome were swept away when he met Martha's mother. Her cry of delight at the sight of him filled the room and she swept him into her arms in a hug.

'Oh, it's so good to see you, Jez. But what are you wearing, lad? You're freezing cold. Why you'll catch your death. Martha run upstairs and run the lad a hot bath and then find something warm of your father's for him to put on. Why a short-sleeved shirt!' she added with amazement. 'What are you thinking of!'

'I came straight from the airport . . . ' Jez said with a shamefaced smile.

'Go on up and I'll make you a cup of tea.'

'Is Luke here?' Jez asked. 'I'd like to see him.'

'He's out with his Granddad, but they'll be back for their tea any time now,' she shooed him out of the kitchen. 'Go and get into some proper clothes.'

There wasn't tea waiting for him when he got down stairs but a bottle of home made wine and the best wine glasses. Martha's father moved across and shook his hand in a firm brisk handshake. 'It's very good to see you, Jeremy. I tried to write and tell you how we felt about your kindness but I'm not much cop at getting things down on paper.'

'Please don't thank me,' Jez remonstrated. 'I was only doing what Dad had asked me to do. Everything was yours by right that came back to you.'

The older man laughed: 'That it

wasn't. It was a scrubby old bit of woodland when I sold it to your Dad and now it is a very well-managed wood with a caravan park and a shop. You didn't have to give those back into the family, Jeremy, it was very generous of you.'

'You lost a lot more than that bit of woodland when the valley was flooded.' Jez said seriously. 'I don't think anything in the world could make up for that happening.'

At that moment Martha came into the kitchen with Luke in her arms and Jez moved across to him instinctively holding out his hands. He stared in amazement at the baby: 'I can't believe it. He's grown up so much, he's almost a little boy now!'

'They grow up so fast. He's crawling now,' said Martha with a proud smile.

'He'll soon be out helping with the animals,' her father added with satisfaction.

Jez frowned with a mixture of disbelief and worry: 'Will he come to me?' he asked. 'I suppose I will be a stranger to him, now.'

'It will be all right, he'll be used to you in a couple of minutes,' Martha said reassuringly as she handed the child over. 'Didn't you once tell me that children and dogs always know if you really like them?'

Jez felt himself laughing with relief and happiness as he hugged the baby to him and felt small hands patting his face. He had dreamt of the moment many times, when Martha and Luke would belong to him. And sometimes, alone in the sweltering heat of the jungle, he had doubted that it would ever happen. That long hot summer in England, the dried up valley, the lost village, had at times seemed like another lifetime. Only sometimes he had found that the memories of that life were more real to him than reality. Now everything was sharply in focus. He felt more alive than at anytime in his life.

'Jez has missed such a lot of Luke's

first year. I don't want him to miss anymore.' Martha said to her parents, her cheeks glowing pink, so that Jez thought he had never seen her look more beautiful. 'We're going to be married, but it will take time to organize and until then I think Luke and I will be staying over at Beckwith Farm with Jez.'

'Well, you young 'uns organize things differently to how we did when we were your age. But if that's what you want it's all right by your Mam and me,' her father said gently. 'We're glad you're getting wed.'

'Let's drink a toast before we have our supper,' Martha's mam's voice was filled with emotion. 'To Martha, Jeremy and Luke. A new family.' And they raised their glasses, in unison, their eyes bright with happiness.

* * *

Before Martha left Moor Top that night she, Jez and the dogs walked down to the edge of the water which shone black and silver in the moonlight. They had made an excuse about wanting to walk off the enormous meal they had eaten. But in truth they both felt the need to retrace their steps to the place where they had met and where their love affair had started. The valley looked very different in it's winter whiteness. There was a sprinkling of snow on the moor and the branches of the hawthorn were whitening with night-frost. Hand in hand, they walked quickly, keeping moving to stay warm.

'The lake came back very quickly once it started raining.' Martha said. 'I wonder if we will ever see the old village again. It's hard to believe in the heat of last summer when it's as cold as this.'

They moved along the side of the lake, and soon the solitary light at Beckwith Farm came into view, shining clear and bright in the crisp air. 'It looks so close from here, doesn't it?' she said softly. 'But really it's a long way away. We'll have to set off soon and get Luke into bed.'

He pulled her close as he said: 'It's only a long way by road. It's not far if you go as the crow flies — across the water.'

'Well, we won't be doing that unless there is another drought,' she laughed. 'And we can walk across the valley again.'

'No, but there is another way. I think, as a wedding present to ourselves, we will build two boat houses and jetties — one on each side of the lake. Then it will only be a two minute boat trip between these two places.'

'Oh Jez, what a wonderful idea!' He wrapped her into his arms and the chill of the night was excluded from the warm circle of their embrace. She kissed him gently, savouring his closeness.

'And then our families will be joined by the water and not parted by it,' he murmured. And she knew that she and Jez would also be joined by their love and nothing would ever part them.

Oblivious to the deepening cold they kissed on and on, until the dogs whined with impatience and they realized their feet were freezing, and so they ran back up the hill together laughing. And, although they did not know it, the sound of their laughter carried in the icy stillness of the night, and echoed across the valley and down the length of the lake, carrying gladness and love with it.

## THE END